SETH WANTS MORE

Seth aimed the flashlight at the entrance to the undersea cave.

The entrance was gone, replaced by a jumbled wall of fallen rock.

They were trapped. Summer felt the panic beginning to rise in her chest again. Seth came over and patted her on the shoulder. He handed her the light, and she directed it as he worked to dislodge the fallen rocks.

He was able to toss aside a dozen small stones. But one huge slab of rock lay unmovable.

Seth tried by himself, and with Summer's desperate help, but the slab would not budge.

Finally Seth pointed to her gauge. Ten minutes of air left. He looked at his own watch and held up seven fingers. In about seven minutes he would be out of air. Three minutes later her own air would be gone.

The thought of those three minutes shook Summer like nothing she had ever felt before.

Titles in the MAKING WAVES series

MAKING WAVES

Seth wants more

KATHERINE APPLEGATE

Pan Books

Cover photography by Jutte Klee

First published 1995 in the United States by Pocket Books

This edition published 1996 by Macmillan Children's Books
a division of Macmillan Publishers Limited
25 Eccleston Place, London SW1W 9NF
and Basingstoke

Associated companies throughout the world

ISBN 0 330 34858 2

A CIP catalogue record for this book is available from
the British Library.

Printed and bound in Great Britain by
Mackay's of Chatham, Kent

For Michael

1

The Truth About Dreams

Summer Smith smiled, enjoying the sight of Adam Merrick as he stood framed by the doorway. "Adam?" she said. "It was a really beautiful evening. The stars, the ocean, the marshmallows."

"And?"

"And you," Summer said softly, remembering so many soft kisses. "Definitely you."

He swallowed. "I'm leaving this minute, and you might just want to lock the door after I'm gone. Because I don't know how long my decent impulses will last."

Summer laughed. "Get out of here."

When he was gone she explored the room for a little while and washed her face. Her blond hair smelled of wood smoke and sea salt, but Summer decided she didn't want to wash that away, not yet.

She climbed into the bed and flipped on the

TV, keeping the volume low, and absentmindedly watched David Letterman play off Rupert, the deli man. In the Merricks' huge house, their mansion, it seemed unlikely the sound would reach anyone. But Summer was in a quiet mood, anyway.

She wondered if this was love. Was *this* how it felt? She certainly felt good, even wonderful. Better than she'd ever felt before. More *in love* than she'd ever felt before.

And yet, was this the real thing? Shouldn't she be able to tell for certain, beyond a shadow of a doubt? Could it possibly be real love if she was capable of asking these questions?

And even now her mind drifted away, to other times, to other feelings. She remembered the warm, powerful sensation that had washed over her when she'd kissed Seth Warner in the airport.

And she remembered the time she'd sat with Diver, watching the sun come up over the Gulf, feeling connected with him in a way that went beyond anything physical. Something she would never be able to explain.

And then, back to Adam, who held her in his arms and made her feel as if the rest of the world had ceased to exist. Adam, who seemed to have an entire world prepared just for her amusement.

Love. Was it possible that she loved all three? Was it possible she loved none of them?

Was it possible she was going around and around in philosophical circles when she should just go to sleep?

Just be careful, she warned herself. It was the number one lesson to be learned from soap operas: true love and happiness were always followed by divorce, insanity, evil twins, or worse. Usually by the end of the program, with a cliffhanger on Friday.

In a more serious way, that was also the lesson of her own family, of her parents who had bravely but never successfully tried to get past the loss of her brother, their firstborn. Perfect happiness was just a warning of trouble ahead.

She closed her eyes and sleep overtook her quickly. Much easier to sleep than to contemplate the great mysteries of the human heart.

She dozed, waking just long enough to turn Letterman off. She slept more deeply. For how long she didn't know. She slept, and dreamed of things that brought a smile to her lips.

A quarter of a mile away, another mind drifted away from the neat patterns of waking thought. A quarter of a mile away . . . and no distance at all.

He followed the dream path as it led him down, down through layers of twisted, dusty memories. He was running through an old, abandoned house, down dark corridors, brushing aside sticky cobwebs, and catching from the corners of his eyes fleeting glimpses of faces he should recognize but didn't.

He knew he was dreaming. He knew that nothing he was seeing or feeling was truly real, not the reality of the waking world, anyway. Was it some other reality?

He knew the house was his own mind, that the corridors were the forgotten pathways buried deep beneath more recent memories, just as drifting sands covered lost cities in the desert.

He followed the truth, or the lie, or the hope . . . back, further and further.

He emerged in the playground, as he knew he would, as he always did in this dream. He was very small. Very, very small. The grass was close to him. Looking down, he could see impossibly small yellow sneakers on his feet. The swing set beside him was monstrous, too big for him.

He was very small.

He had a ball. He looked at the ball as if it might explain the larger mystery. It was cracked, red, chewed-up rubber, as if it had been a dog's ball at some point.

He knew that he would throw the ball. And the part of him watching the dream knew that by throwing the ball he would change his life forever. It filled him with dread and sadness, holding him back. And yet there was longing, too, and the longing made him want to throw.

Strange, he thought, the way life will suddenly reach a fork in the road. Throw the ball and have the life he'd had. Don't throw the ball and he'd have had a totally different, unknowable life.

All this he knew in the dream. He hadn't known it then, when he was so very small, when he had thrown the red ball.

It flew. Pretty far, it seemed. It bounced dully

on the faded grass. It rolled over to the fence. It lay there against the chain link.

A man was standing by the fence. His face was hidden. A woman was in a car nearby, door open, crying. But her face, too, was hidden.

He tried to see the faces, but the more he tried the more afraid he became. He had started to sob, but whether in the dream now, or in reality, or in some zone between the two . . .

The sun appeared.

It had begun to appear in his dreams lately. It was a small sun, a sun he could have put his arms around, and it hovered out of reach, off to the side. Not up in the sky, but close, just a few feet above the grass.

He knew this sun. He *knew* it, but how and where . . . Who was this sun? He couldn't say. But it was someone, and not something, of that he was sure.

The sun watched the scene unfold, unable to stop him from chasing the ball to the fence. The sun had no voice, no arms. It existed, it was real, but helpless.

He ran to get the red ball. He picked it up.

The man reached over the fence and lifted him up.

He floated, helpless.

Helpless while the sun watched.

He woke suddenly, eyes wide, staring into the darkness. "Sunny," he whispered aloud.

But no, that wasn't quite right, either. And now

the dream slipped away, sliding back beneath the cobwebs, fleeing from his waking mind, becoming dusty and distant again.

"Sunny," he said again. Knowing it was wrong, and knowing that nevertheless it had meaning. "Sunny."

Summer was back on the airplane, flying over Crab Claw Key, excited to be arriving. Full of anticipation. Full of possibilities. It was summer vacation in one of the coolest places on earth, and below her spread the sparkling water and the tiny green jewels of islands, strung along the rope of highway like a necklace.

The woman laid out the cards on the little airplane table. She muttered to herself. "Three guys. I see three of them."

No, Summer realized in her dream, those hadn't been the exact words. She knew she was dreaming. She'd always been able to tell when she was dreaming.

"There will be three," the tarot lady said. "One is going to seem so perfect, and one is going to be like a total mystery, and the other one, well, he's dangerous."

"Who are they?"

"Oh, come on," the tarot lady said. "What are you, dense? Can't you see who's who? Do I have to show you the whole future?"

"Would you mind? It would be very convenient to know how everything is going to come out."

"No prob," the lady said. She held up a card, picture side showing.

Summer laughed and clapped her hands. "Oh, of course," she said in her dream. It was all so perfectly clear.

Then she saw the little boy in white. He had begun to appear in her dreams lately. A small, solemn boy dressed all in white. He was sitting just a few seats away. He seemed to be lit by some unknown source, a radiant spotlight that made him glow and vibrate, as if he were not really part of the picture.

Summer felt chills crawl over her flesh. Slowly she raised her hand and pointed at the little boy. "And what about him?" she asked the tarot lady.

But the tarot lady had changed. She had become Summer's mother, slowly, slowly turning to look at the little boy.

Summer awoke, aware of a noise. A soft, barely perceptible noise. She opened her eyes and saw the door of her room opening. The dream sizzled and disappeared, like a television set that has been turned off.

Adam was silhouetted against soft light. He had come back.

Memories of their evening together, warm, vividly sensual memories, washed away all trace of the dream. They had lain together on the small stretch of private beach and watched the sun go down. And they had kissed. Deep, soul-deep kisses that had left them both wanting more.

Yes, she admitted to herself, yes, she had wanted more.

And now he was back, standing in her doorway.

Maybe she *should* have locked her door.

Or maybe . . . not.

She wasn't the same girl who had left Bloomington, Minnesota, to come to this warm, seductive place. This place without rules. Maybe that was good. Maybe it was time.

The answers had come to her in sleep, slipping away even as she tried to grasp them.

Adam sagged against the doorjamb.

From far, far off came a faint, insistent pounding noise.

2

The Incredible Shrinking Adam

dam?" Summer said, tentative, doubtful.

"I could be," he said. It was a voice heavy and slow with alcohol. "You could close your eyes and you'd never know the difference."

In an instant the meaning of what she was seeing changed utterly. She sat up and drew the covers close around her.

"Ross," Summer whispered. "What are you—" Her cousin Diana's warning came back to her. Fear's cold fingers climbed up her spine. *Look out for Ross.* Diana had been strange at the time, almost terrifyingly sad and angry, all at once. *Look out for Ross,* she'd said.

Summer realized her mouth was dry. Her heart seemed unnaturally loud in her chest.

"Thought you might want a nightcap," Ross Merrick said. "You know, little drink before bed.

Help you sleep. Maybe . . . loosen you up a little."

"No, thank you," Summer said, her voice a quivering, uncertain whisper.

Ross came into the room. He staggered and cursed as he banged his knee against the side of her bed.

Summer crept back to the far corner of the bed. She had stopped breathing. Her eyes measured the distance to the door, the possibilities of racing past Ross and running down the hall.

"I'm tired. I'd like to go to sleep," Summer said as firmly as she could manage.

"You don't really want me to leave," Ross said softly. He reached toward her.

Summer slapped his hand away. "Get out."

"Oh, you can be a little more friendly than that," Ross said.

They both heard the noise in the hallway at the same time—rapid footsteps.

Summer breathed again.

"Another time, sweet little Summer," Ross said. He got off the bed and went back to the doorway just as Adam arrived.

Adam glanced anxiously from Ross to Summer. He seemed relieved, but when he turned back to Ross his voice was tight and angry. "What the hell are you doing here, Ross?"

Ross shrugged. "I heard the pounding downstairs. I came to make sure our house guest was safe."

Adam was wearing boxer shorts and an open

robe. His short dark hair was uncharacteristically messy, tufted and flattened by sleep. He stood just inches away from his brother. It was so easy to see the similarity between the two of them. And yet, there were differences, too. Adam was larger than Ross, more muscular, and several years and many hangovers younger. She should have known immediately that it had been Ross and not Adam.

"You're a liar, Ross," Adam said. "You're a drunk and a liar."

Summer was shocked at the venom in his tone. She had never heard Adam angry before. His usual tone of voice was gentle and amused. Now he almost seemed to vibrate with suppressed anger.

"Get lost, little brother," Ross said contemptuously.

Adam grabbed his brother, bunching the front of Ross's shirt between his fists. He slammed Ross against the doorjamb with surprising violence. "That pounding noise was Diana," he shouted. "She's downstairs with Marquez and Seth Warner right now. You want to guess why they're here at two in the morning, Ross?" Adam slammed him again. "You want to try to guess?"

"Get your hands off me," Ross snapped.

Adam hesitated. Then he threw Ross back, as if he were throwing away a piece of garbage. "Get out of here," he said. "Get out and let me clean up your mess. As usual."

Ross straightened his shirt, turned halfway to send Summer a leering wink, and shambled away.

For a moment Adam refused to look at Summer. He passed his hand back through his hair several times. He shrugged, as if trying to shake off the tension. At last he looked at her, then looked down at the floor. "I guess you heard," he said. "Marquez and Seth are with Diana downstairs. They want to see you."

"Why?" Summer was trying to act cool and calm, trying to reimpose normalcy on the insanity.

Adam sighed. "I guess I'll let Diana tell you," he said at last. "You'd better come down or they'll come up here."

Summer climbed out of the bed, feeling conspicuous and vulnerable in her baby tee and boxer shorts. Lying atop her overnight bag was a robe. She put it on, grateful for the sense of warmth it conveyed, though the air was not cold.

Adam kept his eyes on the floor. "Look, Summer, I just hope . . ." He sighed again, sounding like a person who had no reason to hope. "I hope you'll hear my side of things, okay? I mean, before you make up your mind completely."

Summer went down the wide, plush-carpeted stairs, sliding her hand along the polished surface of a carved walnut banister too massive for her to really hold. Adam was a few feet behind her, the two of them a wildly incongruous sight, half-dressed amid the stifling grandiosity of the Merrick mansion.

In the huge common room below she saw Diana pacing, agitated, dripping rainwater from her

12

sleek dark hair, leaving damp footprints on the Oriental rugs.

It must be raining outside, Summer realized. Deep within the hushed heart of the mansion she'd never even heard the thunder.

Diana Olan was wringing her hands like some over-the-top parody of worry. She slapped her hands down to her sides, but they didn't stay there for long. Her usual mask of cool, distant boredom was gone. She looked as if she would scream at the first unexpected sound.

The sight of Diana this way was deeply shocking. Summer had glimpsed *this* Diana only once before, briefly, before the mask had come down again.

Summer looked at Marquez, perched edgily on a couch, wearing too-loud clothing, her buoyant brown ringlets matted and messy, her leg bouncing nervously, dark eyes glancing around the room, as if she were planning her escape. Poor Marquez, Summer thought. She hates getting dragged into other people's psychodramas.

Seth stood, almost completely still, within a pool of shadow thrown by a huge potted tree. He tended to seem serious, even at the best of times, but now he was grim. He looked up at her, saw her, and a slight smile softened his face for a moment.

Summer gave a wave, a small, sheepish gesture. "Hi," she said. This must look like something more than it was, with her dressed for bed and Adam wearing nothing but boxer shorts. She looked around the group as their eyes found her. "Why are you guys here?"

Diana seemed to be transfixed, ignoring Summer, staring at Adam. What was in that look? Hatred? Fear? Even some lingering echo of love?

"What did you tell her?" Diana asked Adam.

"Nothing," he said. His voice was empty of any emotion. Flat. "This is *your* party."

Diana hesitated. She looked at the others, as if they would handle the situation for her. "Where's Ross?" she asked at last.

Adam said nothing, just lowered his eyes and stared down at the floor.

"What's all this about?" Summer asked, growing impatient. The fear she'd felt had lessened. Her friends were here. As ominous as they all looked and as embarrassed as she felt, their presence was comforting just the same. Especially Seth. Nothing bad could happen with Seth there. Seth was like her—an intruder from the normal world beyond Crab Claw Key.

Marquez jumped up from the couch. "Diana, you'd better tell her, all right?"

Diana shook her head. "I just wanted to make sure Summer was okay," she said in an almost inaudible whisper.

"Diana!" Marquez exploded. "You can't start this and not finish it. Look, we're here, right? So spit it out and we can all get out of this museum."

"This is about Ross, isn't it?" Summer said to

Diana. "About you warning me the other day." She could feel Adam tensing up beside her.

"Not *just* Ross," Diana cried, so suddenly she seemed to shock herself.

"What about Ross?" Summer demanded sharply. She turned to Adam. "Adam, will you tell me what's going on here?"

But Diana had fallen mute again. Her hands were working convulsively at her sides. Her eyes were downcast, hidden in shadow. Adam said nothing.

Marquez lost patience. "Ross tried to rape Diana last summer. That's what this is about, Summer. Ross tried to force Diana."

Still Diana was silent. She just hung her head and nodded, almost invisibly.

For a moment Summer didn't react at all. The words just hung in the air. *Ross tried to rape Diana.*

Then she began to see pieces of a puzzle falling into place. The anger in Diana's voice whenever she'd spoken of Adam or his family. The distant sadness she'd so often seen in Diana's eyes. The curt, dismissive way Adam spoke of Diana. The tension that crackled between them whenever they met.

"What happened?" Summer asked. She wanted to go to Diana, put her arms around her cousin, and try to penetrate the wall of sadness that surrounded her. But something was still unspoken. Summer could sense it. The story was not over, not yet.

"Right there, on that couch." Diana pointed. "Adam and I had been out together, dancing. That's

15

right, isn't it, Adam?" she asked, suddenly raising her voice. "Because I have such a hard time remembering the truth, what with so many lies."

When Adam remained silent, she went on. "I was tired. Adam had some friends down from New Hampshire, and he wanted to show them around town. So I said I'd just crash on the couch for a while till he got back. It was a pretty normal thing. Adam and I were close then. I was here a lot." She waited, as if expecting an argument. "Oh, I see— Adam has nothing to say. Fine. Anyway, I was tired, like I said, and I fell asleep. When I woke up, Ross was all over me. He was stinking drunk, but he was still strong. . . ." Her voice faltered.

"I don't think you have to tell us any details." It was Seth, speaking for the first time. Summer had almost forgotten he was there.

Diana seemed grateful. But she plowed ahead in her low, bitter voice. "Most of my clothes were torn. I had . . . he hit me, so I had a black eye." She pointed to her left eye and pressed it tenderly as if somehow it still hurt. "Anyway, that's when my hero came riding to the rescue. Adam came back. He pulled Ross off me. Isn't that right, Adam?"

Adam remained perfectly still, arms crossed over his bare chest, looking down as if vaguely concerned by some pattern in the rug.

"What did you . . . did you call the police?" Summer asked. She felt herself draw slowly away from Adam.

"The police?" Diana echoed hollowly. She

raised her face and shot a look of cold disdain at
Adam. "Did I go to the police, Adam? No, I didn't
go to the police," she said. "How could I? I had no
witnesses. It would have been my word against
Ross's." She made a twisted, bitter smile. "My
word against Ross's . . . and Adam's. See, Adam was
very sorry about what had happened." Diana
slipped into an anger-drenched parody of Adam.
"He was so sorry. He felt my pain, really he did.
But, see, I had to understand how it would be if I
accused Ross Merrick of trying to rape me. See, the
Merrick family, well, gosh, it has so much influence, and darn it if Senator Merrick wasn't the kind
of loyal father who would stand by his son. And
really, after all, what choice would Adam have but
to stand with the family, to deny anything had happened? Good old Adam, my one true love, well,
he'd have no choice but to back up Ross."

Throughout Diana's story, Summer had felt a
growing chill, a grim feeling that seemed to radiate
from her heart and spread over her. She wanted not
to believe Diana. But Adam stood silent. And
Diana's words were too loaded with hurt and be-
trayal and anger and . . . some other feeling. Some
feeling that made her look as if she were being eaten
away from inside.

Guilt, Summer realized. Guilt. Diana blamed
herself somehow. And that lit the fire of Summer's
own anger. She'd seen this kind of guilt before. It
had never stopped eating away at her own parents.

"Is this true, Adam?" Summer asked.

Adam stuck to his silence.

"I said, is . . . it . . . TRUE?" she snapped.

The others all looked at her in surprise. No one could quite believe that tone of voice could come from Summer Smith. Adam looked stunned. His eyes met Summer's gaze, then flickered and darted away.

"It's *still* true," he whispered.

"What?"

"I just told Diana what would happen if she attacked the Merrick family. It's not my fault. It's just the way things are. If she attacks us, we'll end up destroying her. I don't like it, Summer. But I have no choice."

"If *she* attacks *you*?" Summer almost laughed. "She attacks *you*? I think you have it backward, Adam."

But Adam had relapsed into silence.

It was as if he were shrinking before Summer's eyes. As if he had grown small and far away. Miles separated them already, light years, compressed into just a few feet. She almost felt dizzy, disoriented. The world had shifted around her, and nothing was what it had been just moments before.

The silence stretched for a long time. Finally it was Seth who spoke. "Let's just get out of here."

Marquez nodded agreement. "Yeah, this place stinks. It smells like a pathetic little boy who doesn't have the *cojones* to be a man."

"You don't understand," Adam said, almost whispering.

"I think Marquez understands perfectly," Seth said evenly. "I think we all do. Summer? Are you ready?"

Summer looked pleadingly at Adam. Wasn't there something he could say to make everything all right? Just hours before, she had gone to sleep thinking that maybe she was in love with him. Now, in the blink of an eye, he seemed to have become a completely different person.

Then she remembered Ross, leering and drunk at her door. She shuddered. Adam had known what Ross was capable of. And he had brought Summer here, just the same.

"Yes," she said, with a heavy feeling in her chest. "I'm ready."

3

Aftermath and Before Morning

So, I'm guessing no one wants me to put on any music," Marquez said, joking lamely as she started the engine of her parents' car.

Summer didn't answer. No one answered as they drove down the long, winding crushed-shell driveway.

"No, guess not," Marquez answered her own question.

Summer had ended up in the front, with Marquez, thinking only that she didn't want to be near anyone. Marquez would leave her alone. Alone was good at the moment.

Diana was in the back with Seth. When Summer glanced up in the vanity mirror she could see that Diana was leaning against Seth, her head buried in the collar of his shirt. His arm was around her.

Summer felt like a fool. Now that the initial shock was beginning to wear off, she felt like an idiot, like a not-very-bright kid who gets into trouble and has to be rescued by the adults. She knew she should be feeling sorry for Diana, or perhaps raging at Adam, but what she felt most was humiliation. To be dragged out of her bed, away from Adam's house, jerked out of her ridiculous romantic daydreams and be given this nasty, hard slap of reality . . .

Part of her was angry. She knew it was unreasonable of her, but she felt as if Diana had maliciously stolen something from her. Summer had been on a wonderful ride, floating along with Adam. It had been a great story. Here she was, the inexperienced, average girl from an average town who'd ended up going with the handsome, sexy, charming billionaire. It was as close to becoming a princess as was possible in a country without royalty. It was as if she were Princess Di, chosen by Prince Charles.

Bad example. Another unhappy Diana.

Now the big fantasy was over. Crash. Bang. Over.

Even in the soap operas it didn't happen this fast. The reality shift was never this total. How could she have been such a fool? How could she have fallen so far for a guy without ever seeing what he was?

And now Diana was crying in Seth's arms, and Summer had no one's shoulder to cry on. It was unfair. It was . . .

Summer grimaced, angry at herself for having these thoughts.

It was sickening. She was actually resentful of Diana for coming to rescue her. And Diana *had* come to rescue her, despite the pain it had forced her to face.

Summer felt the sting of the humiliation fade, a little at least.

That Diana had come to save her was something not to be forgotten, Summer knew. Not ever.

However humiliated Summer felt, Diana had to feel worse. This wasn't the time for self-pity. She took a couple of deep breaths and brushed off the beginnings of tears.

Summer turned in her seat. She reached back and placed her hand on Diana's arm. "Thanks," Summer said. "Thanks for coming to get me. I know . . . I mean, I can guess how hard it was."

To Summer's surprise, Diana put her own hand over Summer's. It touched Summer's heart. She and Diana had never exactly been close.

Summer's gaze met Seth's. He still held Diana close, offering his shoulder to cry on, knowing that she needed one.

He mouthed a soundless question—*are you okay?*

For some reason, at that moment, the tears she had held back began to fall. Was she okay, he wanted to know? Seth still had another shoulder, if Summer needed to cry about losing the guy she had chosen over him.

Many perceptions had changed in an instant. Diana was not the person Summer had thought she was. Neither was Adam.

And Seth?

Summer looked past him out through the rear window, watching through blurry tears as the Merrick estate, big as a castle, receded into the night.

Marquez dropped Summer and Diana at the Olans' big house, then took Seth to his own more humble house. She parked the big Oldsmobile in the alley behind her home. She closed the car door carefully, not wanting to wake anyone upstairs. All she needed now was for one of her older brothers to start cross-examining her about why she was out so late. Her younger brothers wouldn't care, but her older brothers were not quite as Americanized as she was. There were some habits—overprotectiveness being one annoying example—that they had retained from their child-hoods in Cuba.

Marquez went in through the front of the house. It was a three-story brick building. Her own room was on the ground floor, a huge expanse of territory that had once been an ice cream parlor. She still had a plate-glass display window at one end, and the long, low soda counter fronted by round upholstered stools. Down one wall were the glass and mirror shelves that had once held ba-nana split bowls and milkshake glasses and now held her books, CDs, and assorted bits of clothing. A former hot fudge warmer overflowed with her panties.

The other walls were bare brick, coated by layer after layer of her own extravagant spray-painted artwork. Wild depictions of flowers and bushes and sunsets, and in one corner a tall palm tree that spread its vibrant green fronds across the ceiling. Entwined throughout it all were the graffiti-style names of years' worth of friends and acquaintances, and even a couple of enemies.

The largest name written there was two letters— J.T. Her boyfriend. Okay, ex-boyfriend.

Marquez peeled off her clothes and let herself fall facedown on her bed. She felt a dampness on the edge of the cover, where, earlier, Diana had sat shivering and wet with rain.

"What a night," Marquez groaned aloud. Diana and Seth and Adam and Summer. Jeez. Way too much stuff going on. Too many complications. Too many consequences. Too many tears. Why couldn't people just deal with things and not let them get so complicated?

Summer had been pretty cool. She'd been upset, that was clear, but there was something strong and not easily shaken at her core. Maybe that was the way all the people were in whatever sleepy, boring, party-free Midwest town Summer was from. "They got nothing else to do there, probably, except grow character," Marquez muttered. Summer kept saying they had the largest mall in the world.

"Sure," Marquez said, "no beaches. You got to have a mall when you have no beaches."

She moved back to the counter and shuffled through the messy pile of CDs, some in their boxes, some not, some in the wrong boxes. The Cranberries. Yeah, that was about right for her mood. Something mellow and nocturnal. She stuck in the CD and flopped back on her bed.

No, wait. Wrong song. This was all about not wanting to love someone but loving him just the same.

J.T. stood out on the wall, the letters drawn large, in relief, so they jumped out like a 3-D beacon. She should paint over it. A couple coats of white and it would be gone. *He* would be gone. Him *and* his problems. It would make him disappear from her life.

Except that in too few hours she had to go to work, where she couldn't avoid him. There he'd be with all his scrambled priorities, all his doubts. Another tortured, unhappy fool like Diana. What was it with people? It was easy enough to be happy. Just let the crap flow off you. Just don't let it reach you. What did it really matter if J.T.'s parents weren't his *real* parents? What did it matter if Summer had lost a brother long ago? A brother named Jonathan? Why should Marquez let the two facts coalesce in her mind and form this nagging core of doubt? It wasn't her problem. That's why she had broken it off with J.T.: Marquez didn't need a neurotic, messed-up boyfriend. It absolutely wasn't her problem. Any more than Diana's sick tangle with the Merricks was Marquez's problem. It didn't matter to her. Marquez had her own life and her own goals. She was going to college and law school and on to a life as a respected lawyer. Briefs and motions and hours in the law library.

Tomorrow she would paint over J.T.'s name. Two coats, maybe three coats of white.

She drifted into sleep and dreamed of J.T. wearing his white cook's uniform, emerging time and again from them, covered, then uncovered, flesh materializing, vibrant and real as each new coat of white failed to make him disappear.

Adam Merrick sat for a long time thinking of nothing, leaving his mind blank. His eyes focused without seeing on the huge stone mantel that dominated one end of the room. He didn't want to think. He didn't want to analyze the situation.

Instead his mind wandered back to the small stretch of private beach, where, earlier that same night, he and Summer had sat roasting marshmallows over a fire while the tide threatened to chase them away.

Roasting marshmallows. It was the kind of thing you did with Summer. A simple, unexciting thing. But it hadn't been boring. With her it had seemed transcendently sweet and perfect. It might have been the most perfect evening of his life.

Gone now. Never to be recaptured.

He had cared about two girls in his life. He had gone out with, what? Hundreds? Yes, at least a hundred, here, at the New Hampshire house, away at school, at the parties his father dragged him to. He'd even spent a week in Hollywood squiring a bimbo starlet from a sitcom.

But he'd cared only twice. Diana. And Summer. And both had been ruined for him by Ross.

Adam slammed a fist down on the arm of the couch. Ross. Passed out in his room upstairs now, all the damage done.

How hard would it be to go into his room, take a pillow, and press it over Ross's face? People would say he'd suffocated accidentally, a result of too much booze. Their father would make sure the coroner didn't report anything that would embarrass the family. After all, it was just a year to reelection.

The thought made Adam feel sick. Sick at his own hatred for his brother. His impotent, powerless, pointless rage.

He got up and paced rapidly to the stairs, then ran to the top. The hallway was lined with doors on each side. His own room. His brother's room. The many guest bedrooms.

Yes, Ross was passed out. Helpless. Defenseless. Enjoying a dreamless sleep. Adam knew he would do nothing to disturb his brother's peace. Ross was family. Family was everything.

Adam opened the door to the room Summer had slept in. Her overnight bag still lay on the dresser, open. He looked inside. Shampoo. Conditioner. A brush. A small assortment of makeup, toothbrush and toothpaste. A pair of panties. Socks. Allergy pills. He hadn't known she had hay fever.

Her clothes, the ones she had worn earlier, were draped over a chair. They smelled of smoke from the bonfire.

He would have to return all this tomorrow. He could drive over in the boat. Or maybe the next day.

It surprised Adam a bit to realize it. He'd reached a decision, without even really thinking about it. He was going to get her back. This time Ross would not win.

Adam sat on the edge of the bed. The pillow still showed a crumple where her head had lain.

He lifted the pillow to his face and smelled her lingering scent, a mix of coconut shampoo, vanilla, and smoke. He pressed the pillow against his face. Then he lay back and pulled the blankets over him.

No, this time he was not giving up. Ross was not going to win.

He would win Summer back.

Diana went to her private bathroom and undressed, leaving her rain-damp clothes lying on the tile floor. She adjusted the water to the highest temperature she could stand. Then she climbed in, wincing at the hot spray against her chilled flesh.

Diana slowly lowered herself until she was sitting on the floor of the shower, letting the spray hit her bowed head and wash down over her face.

It was just what she had done that night, a year earlier. She'd sat here, just like this, letting the water pour over her. She had felt powerless and betrayed. She had hated Ross and Adam. And she'd hated herself. The sight of her own naked limbs, tan against white porcelain, had filled her with revulsion.

Diana let the familiar emotions wash over her. It was a ritual by now, one she was familiar with—the memories, and the many layers of "could have," "should have," "why didn't I" regrets.

A year of it. Hoping it would all go away. Realizing it never would. Falling again and again down the long, black hole of depression. Each time climbing slowly back out, only to fall farther the next time and emerge more slowly still. She was losing the battle.

Diana stood up and turned off the water. The mirrors were steamed so that her reflection was no more than a suggestion of pink flesh and dark hair. Good. She hated the sight of her body.

Downstairs, in her mother's medicine cabinet, was the brown bottle half-filled with the pills Diana had counted again and again and again—her security blanket. Her reassurance that there would, in the end, be a way out of the black hole.

But not tonight.

Tomorrow was her day to volunteer at the Dolphin Interactive Therapy Institute. A sad little girl named Lanessa would be expecting her.

So not tonight, though she could feel the black hole opening wide to welcome her in. Not tonight, but before her mother came home. Before then, Diana reassured herself. She would end the pain before then.

4

The Closeness of Stars

*S*ummer lay on her second strange bed of the night, in her second strange bedroom, and listened to all the tiny night sounds that were different here. She wished desperately that she could be down in her own shabby little stilt house, hearing the reassuring sounds of the water as it lapped against the pilings. But the stilt house was a mess at the moment. Seth, who had been hired to fix it up, had gotten a bit overzealous, and for the moment, at least, the house was unlivable.

When Diana had first stuck Summer in the pelican-poop-covered stilt house, she'd been miserable. But since then she'd fallen in love with it. The stilt house was *hers*, after all, and it had the advantage of her mysterious housemate—an indescribably good-looking guy named Diver with no last name, and no place to live except the deck of Summer's little house.

Tonight she had taken the bedroom next to Diana's in the luxurious main house. Diana had refused all offers of conversation or company, and Summer hadn't had the will to push very hard. Earlier Summer had heard the shower running in the next room. Maybe now that Diana had told everyone her secret she would get better.

The pillow beneath Summer's head was firm. Her own pillow, down in the stilt house, was soft. Her pillow at home, a million miles away in Minnesota, was soft, too. There she had a stuffed pink and gold unicorn on the bed beside her pillow. She'd had it since she was four. It had only one eye.

For some reason, sleep didn't come. She had slept an hour or two at Adam's house. Maybe that was the problem. Or maybe it was what had happened after.

Summer jiggled her legs. They seemed to be energized. It happened sometimes when she would be bothered or just too awake to fall asleep. Her best friend from home, Jennifer, called it "wiggle-leg syndrome," as if it were a disease. She'd say, "I'm so tired because I couldn't sleep last night. I had dreaded wiggle-leg syndrome."

Summer threw back the thin covers and climbed out of her bed. Not *her* bed. Someone's bed.

She was still wearing the baby tee and boxers she usually wore to bed. The same thing she'd been wearing at Adam's house as she dreamed now-forgotten dreams.

Her robe was on a chair. She put it on.

The hallway was dark, lit only by a tiny cockleshell night-light stuck in one of the electrical sockets. The hallway was defined by a railing on one side, looking out over the foyer below with its twin curved stairways. The hall took a turn around a bathroom. The other bedrooms were out of sight.

Summer went down by the right side stairs. Her plan was to go to the kitchen, find something containing lots of chocolate, and eat it until a sugar depression put her to sleep.

But once in the dark kitchen, she looked out at the backyard. It was a long, sloping lawn that fell away gradually till it touched the water.

Summer let herself out through the glass doors, out onto the patio. She pulled her robe tightly around her, but when she felt the night air, she laughed. Silly. She had to get used to the fact that "outside" here did not mean "cold." It was much warmer outside than in. The storm that had come through earlier in the night had blown away, leaving warm, moist air behind. She loosened the belt on her robe.

Summer stepped off the patio onto a lawn so lush and deep and springy it was like walking on a mattress. The grass pricked her bare feet, a wonderful feeling. A gentle breeze, smelling of salt and sweet hibiscus. She walked down to the water, stopping at the edge, a low concrete retaining wall just inches above the placid water.

From here, looking left, she could see the outline of the stilt house. It drew her with surprising force. It was amazing how quickly it had come to seem safe and familiar.

She walked a few steps closer, looking for . . . She wasn't sure what she was looking for.

Summer sat down quite suddenly on the grass just at the edge of the water, and lowered her face into her hands. She began to cry, silently at first, then sobbing.

She cried for herself. And for Diana. And even for Adam, so stiff and controlled at the end, looking so trapped, and yet so determined not to escape. She even cried for Seth, who loved her, so he said, and had been there for her when her relationship with Adam had crashed and burned.

At one point Summer wiped her eyes, using the sleeve of her robe. And when she glanced up she thought she saw movement, there on top of the stilt house. A shape silhouetted briefly, then gone.

She took a deep breath and tried to stifle her sobs. But her tears were not yet used up.

Then she heard the soft rustle of the grass very near, and, looking from beneath lowered brows, she saw two bare legs. She raised her sight, glad that in the darkness he couldn't see her red eyes.

"Hi," he said.

"Hi, Diver," Summer said.

For a while neither of them said anything. "I guess you were asleep up on the deck, huh?" Summer asked.

"Yeah."

"I woke you up?"

He shrugged uncomfortably.

"Sorry. It's been a bad night. A real bad night. And the worst thing is, it's just a part of all the bad things." She started crying again. She felt she was making a fool of herself, but that didn't help her stop.

Diver knelt down on the grass, still seeming skittish and bothered. But he didn't leave.

Summer managed a sobbing laugh. "I guess I'm disturbing your *wa*, huh?"

He shrugged again. He seemed about to say something, but remained silent.

"I thought this was all going to be this big party, you know?" she told him, not expecting an answer. "I mean, summer vacation in the Keys, what could be better? Like nothing bad could ever happen here. Like it was all about sun and beaches and meeting guys. But then it turns out there's all this . . . this stuff going on." She wiped her eyes again. "God, Diver, I just feel so homesick now. I just keep thinking about my mom and dad and my room and—"

"Um, look—" he said, interrupting her.

"Yes?"

He fidgeted a bit, then stood up. "Look, come with me, okay?"

She looked up at him, standing over her, wearing his madras swimsuit. It was still, as far as Summer knew, his sole possession in the world. "Why?"

He held out his hand for her to take. She took it. He drew her to her feet and led her down, along the shore.

"Where are we going?" Summer asked.

Diver just made a sighing, frustrated noise. "Just come, all right?"

So she did. They walked past the stilt house, down to where the retaining wall disappeared and a ramp had been cut, leading into the water.

"You'd better take that off," Diver said, pointing at her robe.

Summer did, letting the robe fall on the grass.

Diver led her to the water's edge. It was almost as warm as bathwater on her toes. The temperature of her own skin.

Diver took her hand again. "You *can* swim, right?"

"Of course I can swim. But it's dark."

"It's not dark," he said. "Look. The moon."

She looked, and the moon was riding low, three-quarters full, down over the Gulf.

Summer followed him into the water, feeling it climb up her body, soaking her boxers, creeping up to her T-shirt. At that point she let herself slip, raising her feet away from the sand and shells beneath.

The two of them swam in silence, the only sounds the water and their own breathing. Finally Diver stopped, well out into the water, out past the dark stilt house.

"Like this," he instructed. He lay back, floating with his beyond-handsome face turned up to the sky.

Summer let herself fall back. Water closed over her face, then receded. She spread her arms wide. She could feel her hair fanning out in a swirl.

She looked up and gasped. Stars. Stars like nothing she had ever seen beneath the obscuring lights of Bloomington, Minnesota.

Summer lay there, perfectly suspended. Black water beneath her, going down who knew how far. Black sky above, going on forever. Forever.

And stars. More and more appearing the longer she looked. Too many to count, or even think about counting. Bright, twinkling points of light.

"Do you know that the light of those stars began traveling toward us way back when there were dinosaurs?" she asked dreamily. "They're very far away."

"No, they're not," Diver said. "They're right here."

Summer smiled. Maybe he was right. Maybe it was just like the water. Maybe the water came from clear across the ocean but it was still right there, holding her, lifting her up to float high above the ocean floor, pressing her face up into space.

"Why did you bring me out here, Diver?" she asked. Her ears were under water, and her own voice sounded muffled and far away. Like his.

"You were sad," he said.

"And I can't be sad out here, floating in space and looking up at the stars?"

"No," he said simply.

"No," she agreed.

5

Jennifer, I don't even know where to begin. First I guess I should explain why I'm here and not down in my own house. I went down and got the videocamera because I wanted to talk to someone, and, well, you're still my best friend.

What did I tell you the last time I recorded on this thing? That I was falling for Adam, right? Guess what? That isn't looking so great right now. I'm laughing, but only because it hurts. I mean, I was so, so into him, Jennifer. He's like . . . this perfect guy that every girl would like to fall in love with.

Only, I guess he wasn't.

Sorry. I drifted off there. Just fast-forward through that part where I stared off into space like a moron.

Anyway . . . it turns out there was this whole

thing between him and Diana and his brother, Ross. Ross tried to, I guess he tried to rape Diana, and they covered it up.

All I can say is I feel like a jerk for ever being annoyed by Diana. I didn't realize all the stuff she was going through. And I guess it makes my problems seem kind of unimportant. Which I suppose they are. Tomorrow I'll try to talk to her again, you know, try and get her to go see a counselor or something. But Diana is hard to get close to. She kind of shuts people out.

Seth was there tonight when this whole thing happened. You remember Seth. He's the guy from the airport. The guy I was kind of into before Adam? Of course you remember, I guess I probably talked about him enough on other tapes I've sent you. Anyway, Seth was there, too. He didn't do very much or say very much. He just was kind of . . . *there*.

You know, it's weird in a way, because Adam is a little taller than Seth, and maybe has bigger shoulders, but it was like Adam kept getting smaller, and Seth kept being Seth. I suddenly had this feeling that I'd been a complete moron and made this totally stupid decision.

I don't know. Forget it. Like I said, I'm tired and confused. It's not like I care about Seth. I would have to be the most superficial person on the planet to care about Seth when I haven't even had time to really cry over Adam.

Wouldn't I? I mean, it's wrong, right?

Except, you know, Seth was always kind of

around, if you know what I mean. We did have that thing in the airport, and I know he likes me, or at least he *says* he likes me. Of course, he probably doesn't anymore because I blew him off to be with Adam.

You know what the problem is? I can't ever make a decision and stick with it. I'm indecisive, that's what it is. And you know whose fault it is? That stupid woman on the plane with her dumb tarot cards. She's the one who got me thinking about the *three* guys I would meet. You know, the right one, the mysterious one, and the dangerous one?

Well, not that I believe any of that stuff at all, because I don't—you know I'm not superstitious. I'm just saying it's like, okay, we now have a winner in the *dangerous* category, right? Adam was obviously the dangerous one. Only, it was his brother who was really dangerous. Which leaves the mysterious one and the *right* one. It doesn't take a genius to figure out that Diver is mysterious. There's nothing mysterious about Seth. Which means Seth is the *right* one.

I know, I said I don't believe any of that stuff, I'm just saying—what if?

I feel like I'm trapped in this big web of fate. Like I have no choices. Or else I have too many choices. And I don't know how to deal with it all.

The only good thing is that I never decided Adam was *the* one. What if I had decided that, and then this had happened? But I kept my options open, you know? And now I realize how smart that was, because it would be so incredibly sad to really love someone and then lose him. I mean, I learned that from Mom and Dad and all the years they've felt bad over losing Jonathan.

Yes, I know. That's different. Except not totally.

I want to really love someone and have him really love me. But I don't ever want to lose him. Just think how bad I'd feel if I had decided to be totally in love with Adam. As it is, I feel bad enough. The only reason I'm not boo-hooing right now is that I already did it.

Anyway, Jen, I've learned my little life lesson for the week: Don't get too far into things with guys until you really know them. You have to find some way to . . . I don't know, have some backup, or some insurance or something.

Otherwise, this whole falling in love thing is too dangerous. Remind me of that, okay? You know how I am with retaining deep philosophical insights. Especially when I'm sleepy.

6

Things Always Look Better in the Morning

When Summer woke, she was surprised to find herself in the main house, surprised at all the things that weren't there—the smell of mildew, the lap, lap of water. Surprised at the firmness of a pillow that had given her a stiff neck.

Then she was surprised to discover she was wearing an oversize man's shirt. In a flash she recalled the night before, the terrible earlier parts, the sweet later parts. Her videocamera was on the nightstand. Good grief, had she actually done a video for Jennifer? She'd probably babbled like an idiot. Her baby tee and boxers were drying on the back of a chair, looking stiff from the salt water. She must have found the man's shirt in the closet. Had this room belonged to Diana's father, back before the divorce?

Summer got up, feeling strange and unsettled.

She pulled on her robe, went to the window, and drew back the heavy shades.

"Whoa!" She staggered back, laughing and covering her eyes.

It was amazing. The sun! The sun of Florida, so much more intense than in her home state of Minnesota. The sun *there* was a light in the sky. The sun *here* seemed to penetrate everything, to be reflected back from every possible angle, to fill the world and everything in it with brilliant yellow light. The heat of it glowed from the window glass.

Outside the water sparkled, almost blinding in places. A sailboat was passing by on its way out to sea, big white triangular sails filled with morning breeze. It moved in slow motion, majestic and silent.

Summer slid the glass doors open and stepped out onto the balcony. The balcony was larger than the room, a vast wooden deck surrounded by white-painted rails. The chill of air-conditioning was just a memory in the heat that burned Summer's bare toes and baked her upturned face.

She went to the edge of the balcony and looked down toward the stilt house. It was mostly invisible from here, hidden by trees that ran down to the water's edge, but she could hear the sound of a hammer, pounding, stopping, then pounding again.

Seth. It could only be Seth.

It would be nice to go down and see Seth, she realized. And nice to go back to the stilt house. In fact, as long as the world was this gloriously bright, everything would have to be nice.

Summer went downstairs to make a pot of coffee. It was one advantage of being in the main house. Diana and her mother always bought great coffee. In the stilt house she had a jar of Folgers crystals. Even she could tell the difference.

Diana was already there in the kitchen, looking withdrawn and thoughtful. She was eating raisin toast and leafing indifferently through the newspaper.

"Hi," Summer said, trying to sound casual and normal and not as if she was talking to a delicate person.

"Hi," Diana said. "There's coffee there already. You have to work today?" she asked casually, making conversation.

"Yes, lunch shift. Unless, you know, you want me to stay around here?" Summer poured herself a cup of coffee. "Look, Diana, maybe we could talk."

"I don't think so," Diana said bluntly.

"Okay, then maybe you could talk to a counselor or something," Summer said. "I'd be glad to go with you if you're nervous about it."

Diana made a wry face. "Summer, whatever you do, don't start being sweet to me."

"I'm naturally sweet," Summer said with a trace of sarcasm. "I can't help myself."

"That's better," Diana said. "Listen, when you go down to the stilt house, I have something for you to give to Seth." She slid a manila envelope out from under her newspaper.

47

Summer had a pretty good idea what was in the envelope.

"Tell him for me that he is the original sweet, decent guy," Diana said softly. "I can't go on torturing a guy who'd let me blow my nose on his shirt."

Summer buttered her toast and sat down at the table. She waited for Diana to say more, but her cousin went back to gazing blankly at the paper, occasionally taking a quiet sip from her mug.

"Diana . . ." Summer began.

Diana sighed.

"Look, I really think we should talk about what happened last night."

"Not much to talk about," Diana said. "I put on a big dramatic scene. Now everyone knows just how messed up I am. I'm sure everyone is pleased—that cold witch Diana turns out to be nuts."

"That's not what anyone thinks," Summer said.

"Uh-huh." Diana tried a sneer that became a quivering lip. She concentrated determinedly on the paper.

"Diana."

"Yeah? What?"

"I don't think that at all. I think you saved me."

Diana rolled her eyes. "That's me, a regular Rescue 911."

Now it was Summer's turn to feel reluctant. For some reason she hadn't told anyone the details of the night before. It made her feel vulnerable or foolish.

Like Diana felt, Summer supposed.

"Diana, look. I didn't tell you," Summer began, "but Ross came to my room."

Diana looked up sharply.

"He was at my door, just when you and Marquez and Seth showed up," Summer said. "I thought he was Adam at first. He was drunk. I guess he'd been drinking for a while beforehand. I don't know what would have happened. Maybe you think you looked foolish or something, but that's not how it looked to me." Summer had blurted the story in a quick burst, trying to get rid of it. But the cold fear she'd experienced was not entirely gone. If Diana had not come to the Merrick mansion, Adam might not have awakened. No one might have heard Summer crying out. "Anyway, Diana, I owe you."

Diana was at a loss for words. She seemed to be concentrating, trying to digest some unusual idea. Then, with a small, impatient shake of her head, she said, "Nice of you to say that." She stood up suddenly. "Well, I have to go take a shower."

Summer watched her go and felt frustrated. It was as if what she'd said just hadn't reached Diana. Like Diana had raised some wall of armor that kept out any expression of gratitude or friendship.

"Diana," Summer called.

Diana stopped and turned back, annoyance and impatience clear on her face. "What?"

"Thanks."

★　　　★　　　★

49

Summer poured coffee into two mugs and walked down to her stilt house with the manila envelope under her arm.

The stilt house sat out over the water of the bay, connected to land by a wooden catwalk. It was a modest little bungalow, even a bit shabby. When Summer had first learned that Diana had planned to stick her out here, rather than in the luxurious main house, she had been upset. But now it was home. Funny how quickly it had come to seem familiar.

A pelican sat on the railing, wearing an expression that seemed simultaneously dorky and scolding.

"Hi, Frank," Summer said to the pelican. "How's fishing?"

She knew the pelican's name because Diver had told her. How Diver knew that its name was Frank was a mystery. But then, everything about Diver was a mystery. Last night, as she had finally climbed out of the water, she had been talking to him and only then realized he was no longer there.

Probably he had gone back up to the deck of the stilt house. Probably. Or maybe he was just a figment of her imagination. She smiled at the thought. But no, Marquez had seen him once. So if Diver was a hallucination, he was one that others could see, too.

Summer hesitated at the door to her house. She could hear Seth still hammering away and pausing to sing, then hammering again. A lot was unsettled between her and Seth. An awful lot.

50

He had asked her to go out with him. He had asked her *after* he had kissed her in the airport minutes after they first met. But then it had turned out he had a girlfriend named Lianne. He'd said they had broken up, but then Summer had walked in on Lianne lying in Seth's bed.

After that, well, after that she no longer had any doubts about setting Seth Warner aside. It had seemed so obvious at the time. Seth was a two-timing jerk, while Adam . . .

Right, Summer. You have wonderful intuition about guys. You're the genius of love.

She remembered the manila envelope under her arm. Seth would be glad to get it. No doubt he'd immediately burn what was in it. Which would be a shame, because it really was a very artistic photograph. Diana had taken it the summer before, by accident of timing snapping the shutter at the moment when Seth was rudely pantsed by Adam and Ross and dived for cover off the end of a pier. Diana said she'd been trying to catch the sunset. She'd called the picture "The Sun and the Moon."

Summer put the mugs down on the rail. Yes, it *was* the photograph. *And* the negative. Yes, it was quite artistic. Nicely composed, all the elements balanced perfectly.

She put the picture back.

"That was wrong of me," she told Frank. "I'm ashamed."

Frank spread his wings and glided away, obviously shocked by her behavior.

51

Summer retrieved her mugs and went inside. An impressive amount of work had been done already. The kitchen floor gleamed, covered in shiny new linoleum. It was a real improvement over the dirty, stained, torn, ragged tile that had been there. The hammering continued in the bathroom. There was a smell of sawdust and glue.

Summer peeked around the corner. Seth was on his hands and knees, wearing jeans with no shirt. He had a very nice back. Muscular in a lanky sort of way, with a narrow waist and no fat. She contemplated the view for a moment.

Maybe the tarot lady had it right. Maybe Seth was the perfect guy all along.

Or else Diver was. Only . . . no, he wasn't, somehow.

Or maybe the *right* guy was someone else entirely.

She had to keep all her options open. No falling in love until she was absolutely, dead sure.

Seth had replaced a lot of the old rotting floor with fresh boards, all neatly nailed in place. He positioned a nail and raised his hammer back over his shoulder.

"Hi."

The hammer came down. "Aaaah, jeeeeeeez! Oh, man!" Seth jumped up, clutching his left thumb with his right hand and doing the dance of pain. "Mmmmmaaaan, oh, man, man that hurt."

"Are you all right?" Summer asked, alarmed.

"Mmmph. Hhmmm. Oh, yeah, I'm swell. It's

not the first time I've smashed my finger with a hammer. Which is not to say that I enjoy it." He inspected his thumb critically.

"Is it broken?"

"No, I don't think so." He wiggled it several times, wincing at the pain. He looked at her crossly. "Is that coffee for me?"

"Yes." Summer held out the cup. "Sorry if I surprised you."

He took the cup and tasted a sip. He shrugged. "No big deal. Just if you ever see me using a sledgehammer or an ax or anything, let alone a chain saw . . ." He worked his thumb back and forth.

Summer giggled. "You must have been down here working since the sun came up."

"It's better to start early," Seth said. "It's not as hot then. At least I should have the place ready to be lived in by tonight." He looked down, staring into his coffee cup. "I'm uh, really sorry about, you know, being a jerk."

"What are you talking about?" she asked.

"The way I tore this place up," he said. "I mean, I know it's my job and all, I know I had to do some of it, but I could have been more careful. I could have made sure you could still use the place. Then, you know—"

Summer sighed. "Look, Seth, what happened wasn't your fault. Besides, nothing did happen, so no biggie, right?"

"That's not the point. I can't just be a jerk

because I feel like it." His face was stony. "I was mad at you."

Summer smiled ironically. "Yeah, I kind of figured that out, Seth."

"I know what happened with Lianne," he said. "I mean, I know what you think happened."

Now Summer began to feel uncomfortable. It was way too early to be talking to Seth as if maybe they were going to have some kind of relationship. She had just broken up with Adam—if you could call it breaking up. Summer wasn't sure. She'd never really had a serious boyfriend before. Was what had happened the night before an official breakup?

Maybe not official, but a breakup, definitely.

Seth seemed to sense that he had carried things too far, too fast. "Look, I'm sorry. I keep having to say that. I just meant that I know you're feeling bad, and I wanted to tell you that I still really care about you."

Summer made a frustrated noise. She couldn't deal with this, not yet. "Seth, I really don't think—"

He held up his hands. "Okay, I understand. You want time."

"That's right," Summer said, gratefully seizing on the opportunity, "I want time."

He pointed with his hammer at the floor. "I'll get the rest of the tile laid in here before noon. That way the adhesive can dry by this evening. I'll grout it tomorrow."

"Grout?" Summer grinned.

"Sure, grout. What? What's funny about grout?"

"I don't know, just the word. Grout. Grout. I've never known anyone who used the word *grout* in casual conversation before."

Seth smiled his reticent smile. "I'll try to watch my use of that word."

"No, I like it. It's so . . . you know, so *real*. It's a *guy* word, like *transmission* or *yo* or, I don't know, like *dude*."

"So if I go around saying 'Yo, dude, let's grout that transmission,' you'll know I'm a guy?" He made a face. "Of course, I'd have to be a stupid guy, to grout a transmission."

Summer laughed. "I guess I'd know you were a guy even if you didn't say that."

"I was beginning to wonder," he said.

"What?"

"If you knew I was a guy."

Summer shrugged, feeling embarrassed again. "I may have noticed. I mean, of course, duh." She pointed at his bare chest. "You're really flat chested. That was my first clue."

Now he was embarrassed, too.

"So, um, have you had breakfast or anything?" Summer said, heading briskly toward the kitchen.

"I had cereal when I got up, but that was hours ago," he said.

"I have some eggs and some bread, so I was going to maybe fry the eggs and make toast," Summer said. "Do you want some?"

"Sure," Seth said gratefully. "You know how to cook?"

"Not really, but I'm trying to learn," Summer said. "I have to go to work in an hour, so I need to eat something first. Oh, by the way," she said with careful nonchalance, "Diana asked me to give you this envelope. I have no idea what it is."

Seth looked in the envelope and smiled. "She didn't have to do that," he said. "I'm extremely relieved that she did, but she didn't have to."

"I guess it was kind of embarrassing having that picture around," Summer agreed.

"Hah. You said you had no idea what was in the envelope," Seth said, smirking a little.

"I guessed," Summer said.

"You looked."

"No, I didn't."

"Uh-huh."

"Seth, I'm *trying* to cook. Could you not start arguments with me when I'm trying to cook?" Summer said severely.

Seth leaned against the wall while Summer began cooking. He winced a couple of times, at the way she cracked the eggs and the way she didn't butter the toast all the way to the edges, and again at the way she tried to turn the eggs over too early and broke the yoke, but he stayed where he was.

"I broke only three out of the four eggs," Summer said wryly. "I'm improving."

They sat at the simple round table. Summer gave Seth the unbroken egg.

"Thanks. I was starving," he said, attacking the food.

"Well, all that hard work," Summer said. "Hammering, grouting, and so on."

"Yeah. Plus it was a long night."

"Yes, it was," Summer agreed. He had a smear of butter on his lower lip. It was hard not to stare at it.

"Thanks," Seth said. "You seem like you're okay. You know, about last night."

Summer shrugged. "I *was* pretty upset."

"I wish I could have, I don't know, helped somehow."

"It wasn't your problem," Summer said.

"But maybe I could have helped you, you know?" Seth looked embarrassed now, as if he'd said too much.

Summer picked up the paper towel she was using as a napkin and reached over to wipe the butter from his lip.

"Thanks."

"You're welcome," she said.

He got up from the table, piled her dish together with his, and carried them to the kitchen. She followed him, intending to give the plates a quick rinse.

They collided. The collision lasted longer than it should have.

He put his arms around her. She pushed him, her palms flat against his lean, bare chest.

"I want to kiss you," Seth said.

"Well, you can't," Summer said. "This is just like in the airport. You think you can just go around kissing people when they don't even want you to?"

"I thought you wanted me to," he said. He was still very close. "Are you sure you don't?"

Summer hesitated. Seth took her in his arms again, and this time she did not push him away. He kissed her.

After several very pleasurable seconds, she pushed him away. "I'm sorry," she gasped. "I shouldn't have let you do that."

"You shouldn't? Why?"

"Why? Why? How about because last night I was kissing Adam? I'm not some slut! That's why. Jeez, Seth, you of all people should know. You're the one who's always telling me how people come down here to the Keys and start acting strange and losing control of themselves and doing things they would never do in the *real* world."

"I said all that?" He looked disgruntled. "When am I going to learn to shut up?"

Summer twisted away from him and put some distance between them. What was it about Seth that he could get her to want to kiss him when she didn't really want to? "I have to get ready for work."

"Ready for work? La dee da?" He came close and took her hands in his. "Look, Summer, you can pretend you don't care," he said. "I don't know why you want to pretend you don't care, but that's okay. I *do* care. I'm in love with you. I keep thinking maybe I've lost you, first over Lianne, then over Adam. But you know what? I won't ever give up."

At that moment Summer wanted very much for him to kiss her again. And that realization made her queasy. How could she want Seth to kiss her? Hadn't she learned her lesson about leaping into relationships? She'd wanted Adam to kiss her, too, and look how that had turned out.

"You barely even know me," she said. "How can you say you're in love with me?"

"I don't know. I guess I can say it because it's the way I feel."

"Seth, what if it turns out that I don't feel the same way about you?"

He looked somber. "I don't know. That would be bad."

"Exactly. See? I don't want that," Summer said. "I mean, can't we just take everything slower until we're really, really sure?"

"Slower." He thought that over. "Yes, I guess I can do slower."

"That would be good," Summer said. She was glad he understood. She was not going to jump instantly from Adam to him. That would be wrong, even on Crab Claw Key.

He looked thoughtful, then brightened at some idea.

"So, how about tomorrow afternoon?"

"We could think about starting then," Summer

said, actually a little disappointed that he was accepting it all so well. "We'll take everything slow, see if we get along, see if we have anything in common and all of that."

"After tomorrow we *will* have something in common," he said, grinning wolfishly. "Masks, rubber clothes, and great big feet."

7

Diana Figures It Out, and So Does Lianne.

Thanks, Summer had said. Thanks. The word seemed not to mean anything to Diana. Why had Summer said it? It wasn't as if Diana had done much. On the contrary, she'd frozen up and babbled like an idiot, unable, without Marquez's goading, even to explain why she was there at the Merrick mansion in the middle of the night.

You didn't thank people for making asses of themselves. You didn't thank people for being weak and contemptible. That made no sense at all.

She climbed the stairs to her room. From far off she could hear the sound of hammering. Seth, out working on the stilt house.

Thanks. Like Diana had done something.

She stopped halfway up the stairs, descended, and went instead to her mother's vast bedroom suite. Mallory would be coming home soon.

Any day now. Diana had to do what she'd been thinking of doing before then. Perhaps this afternoon, after she got back from volunteering at the institute.

She went into her mother's bathroom and opened the medicine cabinet. The bottle was there, as it had been on the countless occasions she'd looked. She twisted off the cap, feeling a strange satisfaction in the familiar feel of it. She spilled the pills out onto her palm and counted them carefully.

Yes, they were all still there. More than enough to do the job.

They would find her at the bottom of the circular stairs. She didn't know why she'd chosen that spot. Perhaps it was supposed to be symbolic— Diana, dead at the bottom of the twin staircases, unable to decide whether she should go left or right. It struck her as funny in an awful way.

It would be a small item in the local paper— daughter of famous romance novelist dies from a drug overdose. Dead from an overdose. It would be so common it wouldn't even make the big newspapers.

Although the Merrick family would certainly be relieved.

Relieved. Yes, that was the word. Relieved. Because . . . because they were afraid. Of her.

It was a new thought. A *new* thought, insinuated into the horribly familiar ritual thoughts of depression and self-loathing.

Was it true?

She replaced the pills in the bottle and put the bottle back precisely in its place on the shelf. She went upstairs to her own room.

She showered and was drying off when the thought poked up again into her brain.

The Merricks were afraid.

"So what?" she asked herself wearily. "So what?"

She shook her head impatiently and returned to more familiar thoughts. She wondered when her mother would come home. She wondered whether Adam had laughed at the way she'd stood there, trembling and incoherent. Probably. Why wouldn't he? It was funny, after all, the way she'd stood there unable to do or say anything. Funny.

And yet . . . Again the thought teased her. The Merricks were afraid of her.

"It's not like it matters," Diana said to her steamy reflection in the mirror. She began to dry her hair with a blow dryer, fluffing it with her fingers. It wasn't as if she could actually do anything to change what had happened. She was who she was, and that was the important fact.

And yet . . . they feared her. Adam feared her. Ross. The senator, even . . .

But what could she do? What was she going to do? Get some kind of revenge on them?

She started to laugh.

Then she froze. She directed the blow dryer at the mirror, burning a hole through the steam.

Revenge? Was that the point?

How would that change anything? No, wait, the word wasn't *revenge*.

"Justice," she said. That was the word.

Diana felt a chill that shivered her flesh and thrilled her mind.

Justice. Revenge. Call it whatever. They were afraid.

Her reflection became clear in the mirror, a face floating in a small circle made in the haze. Her dark, sad eyes stared back at her.

How many times had she looked into her own eyes, hoping to find something there? Something other than weakness and self-hatred. How many times had she looked and seen the eyes of a victim staring back at her, a contemptible, weak, disgusting . . .

They. Were. Afraid.

Her hand was clutching the handle of the dryer so tightly the plastic began to snap.

And then Diana did see something new in the eyes that looked back at her. She had already done something to hurt Adam, hadn't she? She'd told Summer the truth, and look what had happened.

Diana laughed out loud, a strange, wild sound. Yes, she had already hurt one of the Merricks with a simple statement of truth.

That's what they were afraid of. They were afraid of the truth.

Maybe they should be.

"Marquez! Pick up! Now!"

J.T.'s voice could be heard clear from the

kitchen, through the swinging doors, over the chattering sound of the precheck computer and above the clatter of the bartender rapidly restocking his glasses.

Marquez gritted her teeth. Oh, J.T. was in rare form today. She hefted a tray of dirty dishes and hitched it in one swift move high up over her head. She barreled toward the swinging doors, stuck out her foot and kicked it open. She slammed the dirty dishes down at the dish station.

"I heard you the first four times you screamed my name!" Marquez yelled.

"I shouldn't have to call you more than once, Marquez. If you weren't off flirting for tips, you'd be here to pick up your food."

J.T. was tall, a handsome, nineteen-year-old blond with calm, mellow-looking blue eyes. Usually. The mellow look was not in evidence right now. His white cook's apron was stained green, red, and other colors that defied identification. He was sweating heavily and looked as if he might at any moment use the fourteen-inch chef's knife in his hand for some evil purpose.

Despite everything, Marquez felt a twinge of attraction to him. There was something cute about J.T. when he was in one of his towering cook's rages.

"You don't need to worry about my flirting." She glanced at her pad and at the dinner plates sitting up on the line. "Hah! The fries go on the pompano, the bake goes with the lobster. Hah. And you're screaming at me?" She added several words in Spanish that made the Guatemalan dishwasher grin. Then she added several more.

Summer, who was nearby ladling chowder into bowls, looked over discreetly. J.T. scared Summer, Marquez knew. At least a little. Summer didn't know him the way Marquez did.

"Don't curse at me in languages I don't understand," J.T. grumbled. He quickly shifted the potatoes.

"Hey, you must not even understand English or you would have gotten the order right in the first place."

"If you'd have picked up your order on time, you'd have spotted the problem earlier," J.T. said, shaking his finger at her.

"Don't you shake that at me," Marquez warned. She tried to look fierce, but darn it, now he was smiling. "Jerk," she said, loading the plates onto her tray.

"Lianne, pick up!" J.T. yelled.

Naturally, Lianne appeared instantly, bustling her tiny, eternally thin, never-even-have-to-think-about-a-diet shape through the swinging door.

"It's so nice working with a real professional waitron," J.T. said, directing the sarcastic comment over Lianne's head at Marquez.

Marquez cursed at him under her breath. As she headed out to the dining room she heard a mock-angry J.T. say, "Lianne, did you hear that?

I wish you'd have a talk with her about her attitude."

Suddenly, Marquez heard J.T. yelp in pain. She glanced back just in time to see that he had burned the palm of his left hand as he reached for a spatula and pressed the side of the oven instead.

At the same instant, Summer recoiled from the bowl she was handling. She raised her left hand and looked at the palm. "Ouch," she said. "I didn't think it was that hot."

Marquez shook her head. No. It was a simple coincidence. J.T. burned himself at least twice per shift, and Summer had been handling hot soup bowls.

But it had happened at the same instant. The same parts of the same hands.

Later, when the rush was over and Marquez could take a break, she hooked up with Summer, who was looking a bit frazzled, leaning against the counter in the waitress station as she swallowed an aspirin with a big glass of water.

"Give me one of those," Marquez said wearily. "Is it your feet or your back that hurts?"

"Feet, back, and all parts in between," Summer muttered. She handed the bottle to Marquez. "And your boyfriend! I hate to say anything bad about anyone . . ."

Marquez smiled affectionately. Summer actually did hate to say anything bad about anyone. "He's my *ex*-boyfriend," Marquez said. "And yeah, he was raggin' big time today. It's because Skeet called in sick, so he's doing extra work."

"Oh. I didn't realize that. Now I feel bad. I shouldn't have gotten so mad."

"You got mad? What did you do, tell him to go to *heck?*" Marquez laughed.

Even Summer laughed. "You know, I have a lot of hostility down deep inside."

"Well, J.T. keeps his hostility right up front where he can reach it easily. It's funny, you two being so different." Marquez didn't realize what she was saying until she'd said it. She gulped hard. Probably Summer wouldn't even notice.

No, Summer might be a sweet blonde, but she was not a dumb one.

"What do you mean by that?" Summer asked.

"What?"

"Why would it be funny if J.T. and I were different?"

"Did I say that?" Marquez took a long swallow of iced tea.

"I thought you did," Summer said, tilting her head and giving Marquez a quizzical look.

"Why would I have said that? It wouldn't make any sense," Marquez pointed out.

"Oh."

"Exactly," Marquez said. Man, that had been close. Close and stupid, she realized as she poured three pitchers of iced tea. It was all a ridiculous idea, anyway. What were the odds that somehow J.T. was Summer's long-lost brother, Jonathan? About a million to one?

Of course, the age was right, so that lowered the odds a little, some relentlessly logical corner of Marquez's mind pointed out. And they were both white. Both blond. And in some ways they looked at least a little bit alike.

Marquez shook her head. This was nuts. It was beyond nuts.

"Guess what I'm doing tomorrow morning?" Summer said. "Scuba diving."

"Scuba diving?" Marquez said. "Cool. Everybody says the Keys are the place to scuba dive. Me, I like air. What are you doing, taking lessons?"

"Yes. From Seth."

Marquez's jaw dropped. "You sleazebag." She laughed. "Boom, out with the old, in with the new. That's my girl, Summer—don't waste any time. I mean, *any* time."

Summer made a face. "It's not what you think."

"No, of course not," Marquez said. "So, what's the deal? You talked to Seth this morning and he did an airport on you?" She leered. Then she realized Summer wasn't denying it. "You *slut!* You let him kiss you?"

"Shhh." Summer glanced around nervously. "He's broken up with Lianne, but there's no point in making her feel bad."

"Speaking of broken up . . ." Marquez grabbed the handles of two pitchers of iced tea in one hand. "The kitchen animals need their liquids." She shook her head. "Little Summer Smith from Horsepuckey, Iowa, can *move.*"

"Bloomington. Minnesota," Summer yelled as Marquez headed for the kitchen. "And it's not like I just met Seth."

Cooks were not allowed out of the kitchen, so waitresses generally brought them something cold to drink at the end of a shift. Generally, when J.T. was working everyone understood that Marquez took care of the duty. That, at least, had not changed since their breakup.

As she neared the kitchen she could hear the sound of rock music. The Ramones were pounding out "Teenage Lobotomy" from the CD player. It was one of the tunes the cooks liked to play at the end of a tough shift, a sort of goof on the intensity of work, shouting out "lo-bo-to-my" with the chorus.

Marquez was dancing before she reached the door, using the iced tea pitchers as a partner.

She backed through the swinging doors, executed a neat spin, and set the teas on the counter. She had both hands over her head and was rocking out fairly fiercely before she spotted J.T. drinking a large glass of tea.

A glass that had apparently been handed to him by Lianne, who was standing nearby, smiling up at him.

J.T. looked at Marquez. Marquez looked at Lianne. Lianne spared a brief glance at Marquez, then returned her full attention to J.T.

"Oh, hey, thanks, Marquez," J.T. said, seeming embarrassed.

"Yeah," Marquez said. "No problem."

She walked back out to the dining room. Lianne caught up with her.

"Hey, Marquez, I didn't know you were pouring drinks, too."

"I do that sometimes," Marquez said. She was steaming, but since she had no good reason to be angry she couldn't let Lianne see it. Let it go, Marquez told herself.

Lianne put her arm on Marquez's shoulder to stop her.

Not a good idea.

"You want something?" Marquez snapped.

"Look, it's not like I was doing anything sneaky."

Oh, no, no, Marquez thought. Like I don't recognize that whole tilted-head, smiling, laughing, admiring-look thing. Like I haven't used it on guys myself. "Oh, I know that," Marquez said poisonously. "I know you're still totally into Seth. Right? In fact, you guys are so tight you're not even worried that he's taking Summer scuba diving tomorrow."

Yeah, chew on that, Marquez thought. Hah. Yeah, hah! Summer told you that in confidence, Marquez, and you blurted it out just because you were angry at J.T.

But to Marquez's surprise, Lianne did not explode. Instead she just looked a little wistful. "Sethie and Summer." She sighed. "I guess . . . I guess I have no choice but to let that go. I was stupid to try so hard to hang on. I guess I'd gotten to the point of thinking Seth was the only guy in the world. And I was upset. But you know what?" She brightened. "Summer vacation will come to an end, and we'll both go back to Eau Claire. Maybe Seth needs his little summer fling. So to speak. And maybe I should follow his example. Why get so upset? This is Crab Claw Key, right? The land of total freedom. The place with no rules. So, yes, maybe I should let Seth go for now, and see what other fun things there are to do."

"Uh-huh. Maybe you could take up skydiving," Marquez said. "Maybe you could try it without the parachute."

"What a good idea," Lianne said, batting her eyes. "Or maybe I could just take up J.T. He's tall. I like tall guys. Do you think he likes petite, slender girls? Or is he just into . . . bigger girls, like you?"

Do not lose your temper, Marquez ordered herself. Do not go off on her, she'd just enjoy it, the sneaky little . . . She took a deep breath. It was all for the best. It was over between her and J.T. It was a time of change. Summer and Adam were finished; Seth and Lianne were finished; she and J.T. were finished.

Time to move on. Time to let it go.

"You want J.T.?" Marquez said coolly. "He's all yours."

Very mature, she congratulated herself as she walked away. Very sensible. When a relationship came to an end it was only natural that people would move on.

Only, she hadn't expected J.T. to be able to move on quite this quickly. Fine. If that's the way he wanted to be, she'd show him some moving on.

8

Not for Sale at the Mall of America

"This will be the day when I finally cross over the line that separates the tan from the untan," Summer said. She lay back on the blanket and contemplated the red glow that came through her closed eyelids.

"This will be the day when I cross the line that separates the chubby thighs from the unchubby thighs," Marquez said, lying beside her, but on her stomach. She looked down the beach, eyes shielded by sunglasses and a green plastic visor. "Because, see, that guy down there with the totally ripped abs is not going to be interested in chubby thighs."

"Don't make me look at guys," Summer groaned. "If I have to roll over I'll get all sandy. Besides, what does lying in the sun have to do with chubby thighs?"

"Oh, fine, so you *do* think I have chubby thighs."

Summer sighed. "Marquez, you do not have chubby thighs. You have perfect thighs. If I were a guy, I'd go nuts for your thighs. No one, in the entire history of the United States, has ever had thighs to equal your thighs."

"So you're saying women in other countries have much better thighs?"

"I'm not talking to you anymore," Summer said.

"Not talking to me? Good. Then I guess I can tell you," Marquez said. "Because if you're not talking to me you can't yell at me. See, I may have kind of accidentally told Lianne you were going scuba diving with Seth."

"I am now officially talking to you again," Summer announced. "*Kind of* told Lianne?"

"As in I definitely told her. Look, I was mad," Marquez explained. "I thought she was coming on to J.T."

"The guy you don't care about," Summer said dryly.

"I don't."

"I see. You just get mad when some girl talks to him."

"Exactly. If I have to be broken up, I don't want him off having a good time somewhere," Marquez said. "So I told her about you and Seth because I just wanted to have something to rub her face in."

"Oh, great," Summer said. "I can't believe you, you weasel."

"I know. I'm sorry. It was pretty low. Not *weasel* low, but pretty low."

"I'm sorry, that was a definite weaselism," Summer said.

Silence fell for a few minutes. "All right already, so tell me. What did she say?" Summer demanded.

"Basically that she was writing Seth off for the summer," Marquez said. "As in she's discovered the joys of summer vacation flings, so let *Sethie* play tag with Summer, Lianne will just play with her new toy, J.T."

"Ouch. Not that you care."

"Or you, for that matter. I think it's pretty clear that I don't care what J.T. does, and you don't really care about Seth."

"This is all well-established," Summer said.

"But I really am done with J.T.," Marquez said. "Whereas you are already lining up on Seth. Adam isn't even cold in his grave yet, and you're scoping Seth. Poor Adam, tossed aside like yesterday's trash. Good-bye, Mr. Merrick. Hello, Mr. Warner. Out with the charismatic boy billionaire, in with the sincere-yet-sexy carpenter."

"I told you, it's not like that," Summer said lamely. "You really think Seth is sexy?"

"Sure. Plus he's a nice guy."

"That's what I thought about Adam," Summer said.

"You think Seth is hiding some darker side? No way. Hey, what about that card-reading lady? Didn't she say one guy was going to be bad news?

And wasn't that Adam? Duh? And isn't Diver the supposedly mysterious one? That leaves only Seth as the right one."

"The one who would *seem* right," Summer corrected. "Besides, I don't believe in all that stuff."

"Uh-huh."

"I *don't*. If I did, maybe I'd have figured out that Adam was trouble," Summer said.

"That makes no sense. Oh, my God."

"What?"

"You might want to dig a hole," Marquez said under her breath. "You know the aforementioned charismatic boy billionaire? He's about fifty feet away and closing in fast."

"What should I do?" Summer asked. She felt panicky, like she should try to avoid him. Yet that was pretty well impossible, given that they were on a public beach. Besides, it was silly.

"Hmm, too bad he's a dirtbag," Marquez said. "The boy does look fine in a bathing suit."

Summer decided against springing up and running like a scared rabbit. The only thing to do was be cool. She'd spent most of her life trying to be cool. Now would be a nice time to actually succeed.

His shadow fell over her. "Hi, Summer," he said.

For once Marquez stayed quiet. For once Summer wished she wouldn't.

"Hi, Adam," Summer said in her squeaky fake-casual voice.

"Look, I . . . I kind of figured you might be here. I stopped by the Crab 'n' Conch and they said you two left right after lunch."

"Yes," Summer said. "Yes, we both left. Right after lunch. The two of us." She was half sitting, shading her eyes with her hand and squinting through one eye. Probably not an attractive look, she realized. Popeye in a two-piece.

"So, um, I was wondering if maybe we could talk," Adam said. "Maybe walk down the beach."

"I guess that means I'm not invited," Marquez said.

"I think we should talk," Adam said doggedly.

Summer hesitated only a moment. She let him take her hand and help her to her feet. They walked down to the water's edge, then along the beach, with just the tepid lip of the Gulf cooling her toes.

"So," he began. "What should we talk about? I wonder."

Summer couldn't think of anything to say.

"Not funny, I guess," he said. He ran his fingers back through his hair and looked past her out over the sparkling green sea. "First of all, I'm really sorry about last night. Everything was going so perfectly, and then it all went down the toilet. Not exactly a great end to our date."

"Adam, I don't think that's really the thing to worry about," Summer said. They were talking like strangers. Like people who had just met. And she did *not* want to do this. She had decided to move on. To get past it as quickly as she could.

"I'm just saying, I hope you remember that things were really great before the whole thing there at the end. I want you to know that I don't feel mad that you left or anything."

Summer almost laughed. "That's very generous of you." There was no sign that Adam heard the sarcasm.

"Since you mention generosity," he said. He reached into the pocket of his bathing suit and pulled out a small, gray, felt-covered jewelry box. It was oblong, with the name of a jeweler in gold letters. Adam opened the box, looked at what was inside, and handed the box to Summer. "Here. I hope this will help make it all up to you."

Summer looked at the box and caught her breath. Inside it was a necklace, gold with a pear-shaped diamond in a simple setting. It seemed unlikely that anyone in the Merrick family ever bought fake diamonds or less expensive gold plate. Which meant that the value of this necklace was probably greater than the sum total of everything Summer Smith owned.

"I know it was kind of an intense scene and all," Adam said, still holding the box out to her. "I just really hope we can go on, you know, get past it."

"Get *past* it?" She made no move to accept the gift. The more she looked at it, and the more the meaning of it became clear, the angrier she felt. Why was he doing this?

"Sure," Adam said. "I mean, there's no reason why this should affect us. You and me. You're not Diana."

"I can't believe you're saying this," Summer said. "I really can't. No reason why it should affect *us?*"

He moved closer now. His face was just inches from hers. A face that she had kissed many times and had wanted to kiss many, many more times. He still exerted an almost magnetic pull over her. She could still recall all too clearly the sensation as his lips trailed down her throat . . .

"Why should Diana's problems ruin what we have?" he pleaded earnestly.

"*Diana's* problems? You make it sound like it's no big deal."

He looked troubled at her reaction. His eyes darted aside, then came back, renewing the link between them. "I don't mean that. I know Diana's been hurt. I wish I could do something to make her feel better, but I can't."

"Sure you can," Summer said. "You can tell her you'll back her up if she tries to do something about Ross."

"What, testify against my own brother?" He sounded incredulous. "Is that what you're saying I should do? I wouldn't even *have* a family anymore if I did that."

"Ross is messed up, Adam. I don't know if he's an alcoholic or what, but he's dangerous."

"He's family," Adam said, pleading. "Besides, give me a break. You think Diana's some kind of poster child for good mental health? She was depressed long before this."

"That doesn't justify anything," Summer said. Her voice was growing louder, to match his. "Ross tries to . . . he tries to rape Diana, and then you, her supposed boyfriend, help cover it all up?"

"My father is a rich and powerful man, Summer," Adam said, almost sadly. "It's the way the world is. I didn't make the rules. I have no choice. I have to stick with my family. No matter what. You understand that."

Summer bit her lip. "Yes," she said sadly. "Of course I do. And Diana's my cousin. *My* family."

At last understanding seemed to dawn in his eyes. Understanding, and pain. Slowly he closed the jewelry box.

"You know what, though, Adam? If someone in my family was like Ross, I'd have to do whatever I could to stop him, even if that did mean sending him to jail. Because sooner or later Ross is going to hurt someone worse, or kill someone even. For his own good—"

"I don't turn against my family," Adam repeated.

"Then I guess we don't have very much to say to each other." She was relieved that she kept the tears out of her voice. She was not going to cry. Not now.

A smile flickered at the corner of his mouth. "You can be pretty cold when you want to, can't you, Summer? Whatever happened to that golly, gee-whiz, midwestern, Bloomington-Minnesota-home-of-the-Mall-of-America sweetness? Suddenly you're acting so tough."

Summer felt the tears welling up. Her throat was

constricted and painful. Her voice was unnaturally low. "I guess you never really knew me all that well."

Adam made one last attempt. He reached for her. "Summer, don't just—"

Quite suddenly, without planning it or thinking about it, Summer slapped the jewelry box from his hand. It flew from his grasp and landed several feet away in the sand. "Whatever it is, I don't want to hear it, you *creep*," Summer yelled. "You jerk. You knew what Ross was capable of, and you put me right in the middle of it. And if he *had* tried to hurt me you'd have sold me out just like you did Diana. So don't go waving some necklace in my face like that means something. You never did care anything about me, Adam. Maybe that's why it's been so easy for me to move past you. And you know what? In Bloomington-Minnesota-home-of-the-Mall-of-America, as you so sarcastically put it, maybe we know what we're worth, and maybe we're worth more than even you can pay."

"Summer—"

"Oh, shut up," she said. She turned her back on him, hiding a face contorted by tears and burning anger and regret.

Diana arrived home from her stint at the Dolphin Interactive Therapy Institute in the early afternoon. She had worked mostly with Lanessa, a little girl whose personal history before coming to the security of the institute was so horrible that reading her case file made Diana cry.

But on this day Lanessa had performed the amazing feat of actually talking to Jerry, one of the tame dolphins. Not just a whispered hello, but two long sentences. She'd told Jerry it was okay that he'd splashed her with water because she wasn't mad at him. It had been a big moment for Lanessa, and for Diana, and even, Diana would have sworn, for Jerry. There was, of course, no way that the dolphins could really understand what was happening—all the professionals at the institute agreed on that. And yet, among the volunteers there was agreement that somehow the big, powerful animals understood everything that happened on an emotional level.

Diana always felt an afterglow from her time at the institute, and today, as she drove the twenty miles down the highway, it lasted all the way home.

Diana parked her little Neon and went to her mother's office. She sat down at the desk and filled in one of the presigned checks her mother had left her. She made it out to Seth Warner. He was almost done with the work on the stilt house, and Diana's mother had asked her to pay him when it was completed. On her own initiative, Diana added an extra hundred dollars. Her mother would never notice it, but it would mean a lot to Seth.

She headed down to the stilt house, intending to leave the check with Summer. Unless Summer wasn't home yet and Seth was still there.

Part of her hoped he was. He had been very kind. Her mind drifted back to disjointed memories of the night before. She had cried on his shoulder—

84

literally. And he had held her. Awkwardly, perhaps, maybe a little embarrassed, no doubt worried that she would misinterpret.

Diana hadn't misinterpreted. She knew he wasn't interested in her. Not in *that* way. How could he be? Seth was from that other world of normal, decent people. People of sun and laughter and easy happiness. People like Summer.

People not at all like Diana.

Diana walked out to the stilt house, holding the check in her hand, waving it like a big, visible excuse for intruding. She started to knock on the door, but it was ajar. She went in.

Seth was right there, his back to her, absorbed in something. A book.

Good grief, a school yearbook. Summer had brought her school yearbook with her. Diana almost laughed. Yes, Summer was a different variety of human being. And so was Seth, concentrating so closely on what was, undoubtedly, a grainy, badly done black-and-white picture of Summer.

Diana drew back outside. She sighed. She shouldn't feel disappointed. Of course Seth was in love with Summer. Of course he was. How could he not be?

A pelican (named Frank, Summer insisted) swept in, wings beating the air. He settled on the railing.

"True love," Diana whispered to Frank. She peeked around the corner. Seth was seated at the table now, the better to admire the yearbook photo.

He had a wistful half-smile and was running his finger over the image. It made Diana want to cry. It would be a wonderful thing to be loved that way. A really wonderful thing.

Had Diana ever been loved like that? Had Adam once longed for Diana the way Seth longed for Summer? Diana smiled ruefully. Hard to imagine anyone feeling that way about her.

She knocked on the doorjamb. Seth jumped, startled. He flushed, looking guilty, and snapped the book shut.

"Just me," Diana said. "You can continue drooling."

"I don't know what you're talking about," Seth said as though he actually expected her to believe him.

"Uh-huh. I have a check for you." She flourished it and put it on the table for him.

"Well, I still have a few things left to do around here," he said.

"Anything that will give you an excuse to be around Summer," Diana said.

He didn't answer. Instead he changed the subject. "It was nice of you to give me back the picture."

"Have you burned it yet?"

"No. I won't, either. It's a nice photograph— even if it is the most embarrassing thing in my life. You were always talented with a camera."

"Thanks," she said.

"So, um, how are you doing?"

She shrugged. "It's all ancient history," she lied. "Old news. I don't even know why I was weeping last night. Probably just an excuse to get to slobber all over you and make Summer jealous."

"I don't think we're at the point where she'd be jealous of me," Seth said sheepishly.

"Well, you obviously are, even if she isn't," Diana said, pointing to the yearbook.

He had no answer, just looked even more sheepish. Diana started several times to say something. What she wanted to say was *Seth, any girl who doesn't want you is a fool . . .* or *look, if it doesn't work out with Summer . . .* or just *it would be nice to think that your shoulder would be there for me again, the next time I need to cry . . .*

But all of those things would be the wrong things to say.

Instead she said, "You realize, of course, that I kept one copy of the picture."

Seth laughed silently. "No, I don't think you did."

"No, I didn't," Diana admitted. "Seth, how come . . ."

"How come what?"

She'd been about to say "How come we never went out? How come I never realized what a great guy you are? How come you never fell in love with me?" But she knew the answer. Seth could not be the person he was and love a person like Diana.

"Never mind. Enjoy the check."

"Diana? I know this is none of my business, but

are you thinking of doing anything about Ross? I hate to see him get away with what he did."

Diana smiled. "What should I do?"

"I don't know," Seth admitted. "I guess I'd like to see you get justice."

Diana nodded thoughtfully. "What's the difference between justice and revenge?"

Seth shrugged. "I'm not sure, Diana."

"Me neither," Diana said. "But I'm thinking about it."

9

Black Rubber and Blackmail

*O*kay, now you see why you use powder on the inside, right? So it will slide on easier," Seth explained patiently. His upper torso was already encased in black and blue rubber. He stood with arms crossed over his chest, shaking his head critically.

Summer was making a spectacle of herself, trying to get her hand through the sleeve of the wet suit top. Her hand was stuck, and with every push or pull the rubber just stretched, with the result that she'd ended up turning in a circle trying to accomplish the simple act of getting dressed.

It would have been bad enough if only Seth had been there to watch her fight her idiot battle against the rubber, but they were at the end of the public beach, not far enough from afternoon sunbathers, several of whom were staring at her with frank amusement.

"Wasn't there somewhere more private we could have done this?" Summer demanded, grunting as she at last popped her hand through. "Finally. Of course, I'll never be able to get it off."

"The only other choice was in the bay, and that's no fun. Too much old crap, thrown-away tires, and old shoes and stuff in that water. Besides, over there you have all the tourists hot-rodding around in their rented motorboats."

"And on that side I might not have had to do this in front of a thousand people," Summer grumbled.

"Ignore them," Seth advised.

"Why is this even necessary? The water here is hot, and the suit makes me feel like I can't breathe."

"The water's not as warm deeper down," Seth advised. "Besides, it's just the top. Be grateful you aren't wearing the pants, too. Now, *those* are hard to put on." He smiled. "I think you look kind of sexy this way."

"Very funny. I'm burning up. Anyway, we're not going deep, are we?" She added the last part nervously. The fact that she was going to be breathing *under* the water was something she had avoided thinking about.

"No, not deep. I just want you to learn everything in the right order. Weight belt," he said. He lifted a heavy belt studded with lead weights and leaned close to wrap it around her waist. "Normally we'd use a buoyancy compensator—"

"Oh, I love those," Summer joked.

"Only, Trent didn't have any spare to lend out. Okay, now, the tanks. Turn around."

Seth hefted a single gray metal tank onto her back, helping her work her arms through the straps. It felt as if it weighed a hundred pounds. "I'm going to drown in all this."

"No, you won't drown. I won't let you drown. You have your mask? Put it on your head but don't pull it down yet."

"Yes, master," Summer grumbled. "At least that way no one will be able to recognize me. The whale girl. Free Willy. The newest attraction at Sea World."

"Snorkel?"

"No thanks, I don't snorkel. It's an unhealthy habit. I gave it up."

"Very funny," Seth said, smiling. "But not as funny as the next part. Go ahead and put on your fins."

"On my feet?"

"No, on your ears. Of course on your feet," Seth said. He handed the huge, triangular flippers to her.

"My feet are all the way down there," Summer said, pointing. "I can't move, let alone bend over."

"I'll help you. This time."

He bent down and fitted the fins on her feet. Then he stood up.

"Why is it that you look like James Bond or something," Summer asked, "whereas I feel like Oprah *before* the diet?"

"You just have to get used to it. Besides, you look great."

"We're going to die, aren't we?" she asked.

"Eventually. Not today, though. Knock on wood."

"I don't have any wood."

"Oops."

"Oh, you're really funny," Summer said.

"Since we don't have any wood, how about a kiss for luck?" Seth said.

"In front of ten million people who are already trying not to laugh at me?" Not that she didn't want to kiss him. She'd been thinking about it much of the afternoon as he solemnly went through all the instructions she needed, being so serious that his very seriousness had started to seem funny.

"You want *bad* luck?" Seth asked.

"This is total blackmail," Summer grumbled. But she tilted back her head, lips parted, eyes drifting closed. The memory of their kiss over eggs had lingered. It had been an excellent kiss. And it wouldn't mean she was getting too deeply involved with him or anything. It was just for luck.

To her annoyance, Seth planted a brief, light kiss on her forehead.

"We don't need *that* much luck," he said, obviously hugely amused by himself. "Come on." He led the way the few feet to the water's edge. "Now, remember everything we talked about. All kidding aside, it's fairly easy to screw up, so do exactly what I tell you."

"You'd like that."

Flopping across the sand on her monstrous flippers, Summer made a face at Seth's back. Water washed over her toes, which just made walking in fins even more difficult.

"Okay. Time to get wet," he said after they had walked out a way. "Let's do it."

The first sensation was of drowning. Definite drowning. Summer sucked wet air through the snorkel in quick, panicky gasps. She couldn't see anything at all.

Of course, that was because her eyes were shut.

Summer opened her eyes and nearly screamed. Her head was definitely underwater. She was breathing, but her head was underwater.

Okay, it wasn't exactly deep water. Actually, the sandy floor of the Gulf of Mexico was only about two feet below her.

She sucked air through the snorkel again. A small wave broke over her and she caught a sickening mouthful of salty water. She swallowed it, and only then remembered that Seth had told her to spit it out and then clear her snorkel.

Great. Now she was going to die from drinking salt water. Everyone knew you couldn't drink salt water.

Summer felt something tapping her on the back of the head. She looked up, raising her mask out of the water.

Seth was standing in front of her, grinning.

"Takes getting used to, huh? Breathing underwater and all?"

"Ung gwesh sho," Summer said. Then she spit out the snorkel mouthpiece. "I guess so."

"Okay, we're going to go out a little farther. You'll swallow less salt water that way. By the way, there's no shortage of oxygen on the planet. You don't need to try to breathe it all at once. Easy does it."

"We're not going out *too* far," Summer said anxiously.

"Summer, the water is so shallow here that if we swam out a quarter mile we'd barely be in ten feet."

"Oh."

"Follow me, now. I'll be just a little ahead of you, okay? And I won't let anything happen to you."

"Okay."

She stuck her mask under water again, this time keeping her eyes open, and tried to breathe normally. It took a while till her breathing became anything like normal, but eventually it did. She learned to clear her snorkel when a gulp of seawater poured in. She learned to swim by moving her legs slowly, powerfully, letting her fins do part of the work.

Gradually, very, very gradually, the sandy floor of the Gulf fell away. Two feet. Three feet. Four feet. She glanced over at Seth, arms trailing casually at his side, legs working regularly. He looked at her every few seconds, checking to see that she was okay, his eyes looking overly intense behind the mask.

It wasn't the worst feeling in the world, the way

he was so concerned. It did make her feel safe. And he was so obviously at home out here.

Kind of ironic, Summer thought. She'd gone floating at night with Diver, but she was diving with Seth. Somewhere in there was irony, she wasn't sure where.

Seth reached over and took her arm gently, signaling her to stop. They both came to rest, and Summer stood up.

Only, the Gulf floor wasn't four feet below her. It looked like four feet. But it was at least six, which was unfortunate, since that left all of Summer underwater.

She gasped and fought her way back to the surface. Seth put his arms around her. Summer spit salt water directly in his face.

"Oh, sorry! Oh, gross," she cried.

Seth laughed. "It's okay. I was already wet."

"Yeah, but I spit on you. I thought it was more shallow." She was chattering, not from cold, but from the shock of discovering she was so far out in the ocean. She twisted back and forth to try to find the land. It was harder treading water with tanks and a weight belt, though the wet suit top seemed to give her some buoyancy.

"We're only about a hundred yards out," Seth reassured her.

"How come I can't see the beach?"

"Because it's behind you." He turned her around, held her by the waist, and boosted her up to see over the crests of the tiny waves.

"Oh." Beach umbrellas could be seen very clearly. Parallel with her, a small boy rode an inflated air mattress. They had not exactly swum all the way to Bermuda.

"Okay, ready to try going on the regulator?"

"I guess so," Summer said gamely.

Seth went back over a list of all the things he'd told her on land, making sure she understood everything she had to do.

"By the way, *now* we need more luck," he said.

"I'll drown," she said.

"No, you won't." He put his arms around her, or at least as far as he could with the bulky tank on her back. This time he really kissed her and she kissed him back, a salty, strange, intense kiss. He held her on the surface by powerful strokes of his fins, buoying her. She put her arms around his neck, feeling at once exposed and invisible in the trough between gentle swells.

"Now we'll have plenty of luck," he said.

"You're sure this is part of the training?" Summer asked, trying to sound flip, but with a slap of water in the face, gargling instead.

Finally, when she was ready, he helped fit the regulator mouthpiece in her mouth. It was a little like doing the kindergarten trick where you shove an orange peel over your teeth.

"Ung mung lnk hrnhy nhad," she said.

"Did you ask if you looked pretty silly with that thing in your mouth?"

Summer nodded.

"The answer is yes. Come on. See you below."

Summer tested the air coming through the regulator. It seemed like normal air.

She stuck her head under the water and let herself sink slowly down. Seth was already below her, looking up protectively. She began to swim, slowly descending toward him.

Now, this! This was cool, Summer thought. Okay, this was definitely cool. Much cooler than drifting around on the surface with the snorkel.

I am underwater!

She did a slow roll over onto her back and looked up at the surface of the water. A brilliant yellow sun was nearly blinding, even through the ripples of the sultry waves. She exhaled an explosive cloud of bubbles and watched them rise, circling and bobbing and sparkling in the sunlight.

Her mind went back to the night with Diver, watching the stars overhead, floating motionless between sea and space. And before that she had looked out over this same sea with Adam, skimming across it in his boat. Now here she was with Seth, encased in protective rubber armor, literally beneath the waves, invading an alien world, a vast new undiscovered universe.

She was sure there was some profound meaning there somewhere.

She touched the bottom and trailed her hand through the sand, stirring up a tiny whirlpool. Okay, Summer thought jubilantly, now summer vacation is back on track.

This would be fun with anyone, she told herself. It's not because I'm with Seth.

Seth floated by, paused, and waved his hand in a slow, beckoning gesture that meant "follow me."

He was leading her deeper. She hoped he wouldn't take her too deep.

"Look, you *have* to come," Summer insisted. "I want to get some stuff to go on my walls. I have brand-new linoleum and brand-new tile and even brand-new grout, and all I have on my walls is nothing. Besides, I need a book about fish."

Summer and Marquez were on the lawn with Diana, who wished they would go away. Marquez was just back from work, flush with tip money. Summer was back from scuba diving and had not shut up about it yet. The two of them had already changed into mall-crawling clothes. They stood over Diana, who was lying on a beach chair under two layers of sunscreen, baking and thinking.

"Yeah, we really, really want you to come with us," Marquez said. "Really."

Diana shook her head wearily. "Let me guess. Marquez can't borrow her parents' car, and you both need a ride."

"You shouldn't be so cynical," Summer chided.

"Yeah. You're right, we do need you to drive, but still, cynicism isn't called for," Marquez said.

Diana nodded thoughtfully. "Summer, do

you happen to have one of those little, tiny tape recorders?"

"What? Why?"

Diana looked bored. "I need one, okay?"

"I don't have one," Summer said.

Diana climbed to her feet. "Well, then I guess I'll just have to buy one. Which means I'll drive you to the mall. Give me a minute to change. If you want, we can take Mallory's Mercedes. The keys are on a hook in the pantry. Why don't you two get it out of the garage and put the top down."

"How does she manage to do that?" Marquez asked Summer. "Make us feel like we're her servants."

"Or you can walk to the mall," Diana said over her shoulder. "It's only like twenty miles."

Diana changed quickly into a patterned sarong skirt and a white top. She was on her way out of the house when the phone rang. She picked it up in her mother's office.

"Yes."

Her heart sank as she recognized her mother's voice. "Diana, I can't believe you're there. I expected to get the machine."

"Sorry to disappoint you. You're not back, are you?"

"No, honey, I'm in Sacramento. California. Don't even ask. They've extended the tour, and I have to go on talking about this silly book for another week."

Diana breathed a sigh of relief. It was a reprieve.

So much had gotten tied up in her mind with the return of her mother. Another week to decide what to do. "Well, I guess I'll survive."

"I know *you'll* survive. How is Summer?"

Diana rolled her eyes. "She's fine. As a matter of fact, I'm taking her shopping. The stilt house is almost all fixed up."

Diana heard the honking of the Mercedes's horn outside and the faint sound of Marquez shouting something impatient. "She's waiting. I better go."

"Okay. You still have my ATM card and the credit cards?"

"No, I've been supporting myself by picking up sailors."

Her mother made a phony laugh. "That would be unusually outgoing for you, Diana. It's nice to know you're meeting people."

"Uh-huh. Are we done?"

"Yes. Buy something nice for Summer, a gift from me. And get something for yourself, too."

Diana hung up the phone, seething as she did after almost any interaction with her mother. Her gaze fell on a small framed photograph on her mother's desk. It showed Mallory, back before she'd become a big success, back when her hair was still normal-size, before it had become romance-writer hair. She'd never noticed the picture before. In it, her mother seemed unusually frumpy. And it wasn't even a good picture, all fuzzy and off-center.

Then it occurred to Diana that the picture was

there for a reason. This was Mallory's "before" picture. It was to remind her of what she had been and what she had become. On the wall, much larger, gilt-framed, was the publicity shot from her mother's first bestseller. A whole new Mallory Olan.

Before and after.

Diana could imagine her own "before" picture. It would be a picture of her now. Right now. *This* was the before.

Suddenly she took out her mother's address book. The number was bound to be there still. They'd done a little puff piece interview with Mallory . . . yes. There it was.

She could do it. She could do it right now. The idea excited her in a dark, unsettling way. Yes, why wait any longer?

It was all so new. The entire concept of doing anything at all was new. It had been so long. So much time had passed when all she had managed to do was wallow in depression and dream of how she would end her suffering.

Some new energy was inside her now. She could feel it. But it was fragile force, like a single candle in the darkness that her life had become. She wanted to nurture that candle, keep it safe from blowing winds that might snuff it out.

Start it now.

The great dark hole of depression was still there, still tangible and real and oddly seductive. Against it just the one small light. She had to make it grow, give it air and fuel. To let the fire burn brighter and hotter, until it dispelled the last of the shadows.

Yes, start it *now*.

She checked the number again. But she didn't dial it. Instead she called a different number. Area code 202, Washington, D.C.

She took a deep breath. "Start it, Diana," she ordered herself sternly. "Do it now, or you'll find one excuse after another never to start."

She dialed the phone number. There was a delay, then it rang.

Click.

"Senator Merrick's office."

"I wan—" Diana's voice choked off. She almost crashed the receiver down in panic but stopped herself. She cleared her throat. "I want to speak to Senator Merrick."

"I'm sorry, but the senator cannot take calls. I'll be glad to take a message."

"No," Diana said sharply. "He will want to take this call himself. It's personal. It's about his son."

A long pause. "Who's calling?"

"My name is Diana Olan. Tell Senator Merrick to take this call. Or—" She hesitated. Her prepared speeches all sounded silly now. Like something a child would dream up. "Look, tell him if he doesn't want his son to go to jail, he'd better take this call."

An even longer pause. Then, "Please hold."

Outside, the car horn honked again, more

insistent. Diana could picture Marquez and Summer out there, playing the stereo, talking away, getting annoyed that Diana was keeping them waiting.

And she could picture another scene, over a thousand miles away in Washington. She imagined a dark, paneled office. Maybe the Washington Monument was visible from the window. Maybe—

"Who is this?" A brusque, haughty voice, instantly recognizable.

"Senator Merrick?"

"Yes. Now, what do you have to say? I'm a busy man."

"Your son tried to rape me." The words came tumbling out, all of their own accord.

"Don't waste my time. I'm hanging up."

"I'll go to the police," Diana said.

"Do whatever you think you have to do, young lady," he said calmly. He even sounded a little bored.

But no, he wasn't bored, Diana knew. "Senator, your son Ross tried to rape me in your Crab Claw Key home last year. I know you heard about it. I know Adam told you what happened. That's why you put Ross through rehab."

"I know who you are, Diana. But I thought you were a smart girl," he said contemptuously. "I thought you knew better than to try to blackmail me."

"It isn't blackmail," Diana said. "I'm just . . . It's just that . . . I'm tired of being afraid."

"No one has tried to threaten you," he said. "You invent some incident and call me up—"

"I didn't invent anything and you know it!" Diana cried.

"So, you have witnesses? The police will want to know if you have witnesses."

"I realize that, Senator. I know the police will want witnesses. And I know Adam will lie to protect Ross. But you know what? I figured something out. The police may want witnesses, but there are other people who may not care all that much whether I have a witness or not."

"I think this conversation has gone on long enough."

"I have a number I want to give you. Write it down. And when you hang up, call them." Diana read off the phone number. At the other end she could hear a pen scratching on paper.

"Call that number, Senator Merrick. And then I want to meet with you, face-to-face, down here."

"What is this number supposed to be?" the senator demanded.

"It's the number for *Inside Edition*. You know, the tabloid show. The one that would be really interested in this kind of a story."

The only sound was that of a breath, sharply inhaled, then let out slowly, shakily.

"All right, young lady," the senator said at last. "You want a meeting? I'll be down on the island early next week. I'll have someone call you. But you want to be careful about trying to blackmail me."

"It isn't blackmail."

"Of course it is," he said, sounding weary and cynical.

"Call it whatever you want, then," Diana said. Slowly she replaced the receiver in its cradle. "I call it justice," she whispered to herself.

Outside, the horn now blared in one long sound. Diana grinned. Shopping. Why not? She did have certain purchases to make.

10

I'm sorry, I'm sorry, I'm sorry, I know it's been a long time since I recorded anything for you. Like a week, I guess. No, wait, more than a week. But it's been kind of a busy week.

For one thing, this waitress at work quit, so I've picked up some of her shifts. I'm doing dinners now sometimes, which is good because the tips are a lot better. The other night I made eighty-two dollars. Of course, my feet were killing me afterward, and I pulled a muscle in my back lifting this one tray. But Seth gave me an excellent back rub after work. . . . Oh, wait. You don't know anything about all that, do you?

Seth and I are kind of going out sometimes. The thing is, we've both agreed that we can still see other people if we want, and we're not like capital "B" boyfriend and capital "G" girlfriend. We would be more lowercase boyfriend and girlfriend. We do things together, but I'm still very cool and in control about it.

Not that I'm seeing anyone else. It's just that I could if I wanted, and I probably will, because I have totally learned my lesson about falling in love with people too soon and getting hurt when it turns out they're dirtbags. I wouldn't mention any names. Especially any names that start with "Ad" and end with "am." Did I tell you he tried to give me this necklace? Like I would just forgive everything for gold and diamonds.

Okay, yes, I thought about it. But I said no. You'd probably agree with Marquez that I should have taken the necklace and *then* blown him off. Marquez got so mad at me she was yelling at me in Spanish. The only Spanish she ever speaks are four-letter words, or maybe they're five letters in Spanish. Of course, she wasn't serious. Maybe.

But speaking of Marquez, she's still broken up with J.T. Only, the other day she saw him making out with Lianne in the walk-in, and she was very upset over that, because that's where she and J.T. used to make out when they were at work. She tells me every day how she's totally over him, and then spends an hour muttering and grumbling under her breath about him and Lianne. Now she says she's going to get a new boyfriend. I'm not kidding—she's on the look-out for someone even better-looking than J.T. so she can rub his nose in it. She painted out J.T.'s name on her wall, which is as serious as Marquez gets.

And as for Diana, I don't even know. I tried to talk to her a couple of times, but she's still as private as ever. Although, it's funny, because she *is* different. I mean, before you'd talk to her and there was always this feeling about her, like she was thinking about something else. Well, she still is that way, but it's as if what she's thinking about has changed. She has this look, like she's planning something. You know, like she's a secret agent or something. I don't know how to explain it any better than that.

Diana says Mallory, her mom, is coming home soon. Her book tour got extended, but she'll be back any day now. Maybe that will help.

Anyway, tomorrow I get certified.

Ha, ha, Jennifer, no, not certified insane. Very funny. Jennifer, I *so* know the way your mind works.

I'm getting certified as a scuba diver. Seth has been teaching me, and Jennifer, it is the most excellent, coolest thing on earth. You have *got* to learn, so we can go together when I get home. I'm serious—we can dive in lakes. Seth says lakes are boring, but you could learn there, and even when all you see is sand, which is all I've really seen, it's still way cool.

I'm feeling like things are going more normally now. Like all this stuff with Adam was just this unhappy phase. From now on, it's just happy happy, joy joy for the rest of the summer.

On the other hand, I have this other feeling that things never stay simple for very long. Like on *The Young and the Restless*. Anytime everyone is happy, you just know that a murder or a divorce or a long-lost daughter is going to show up by the end of the show.

So tune in tomorrow, for more of *The Tan and the Clueless*.

11

All About Seeing and Not Seeing Guys

O kay, now smile," Summer directed. She pointed the video camera at Seth, who was standing there, sullen, thumbs hooked in the waist of his jeans, refusing to cooperate.

Summer lowered the camera. "Would it kill you to smile?"

"I don't even know this Jennifer person," Seth grumbled.

"She's my best friend. And she just sent me a tape of *her* boyfriend. I mean, this guy she's sort of seeing, anyway," Summer amended quickly. "I don't know if he's actually a boyfriend."

"So now you want to be able to show her your *guy you're sort of seeing, anyway?*"

"Yes," Summer said. "I want her to see what you look like."

"Uh-huh. Have you taped Diver yet?"

"No. That's not the same," Summer said impatiently.

"Why not?"

"Because Diver is not a guy I'm sort of seeing, you are," Summer explained. Lately Seth had been trying to meet Diver. Like he was jealous of Diver, which made no sense at all. "See, Jennifer shows me the guy she's sort of seeing, and he's cute and all, so now I have to show her the guy I'm sort of seeing so she'll realize that the guy I'm sort of seeing is cuter . . . almost as cute . . . as the guy she's sort of seeing."

Seth just stared at her. "If two guys were doing this, you'd say it was sexist." Then, under his breath, but loud enough for Summer to hear, "*Almost* as cute." He shuddered. "*Cute* is such a girl word."

"Like *grout* is a boy word. You have *grout*, we have *cute*. Just like you boys have belching and grunting, and we have actual conversation."

"Ugh," Seth grunted. "Camera no good. Camera scare caveman." He took the camera from her hands. "Caveman need to be bribed." He wrapped his arms around her and kissed her.

Summer let him draw her down onto her bed. He lay on his back. She lay atop him, kissing his lips, enjoying the feel of his hard body. Then she noticed a familiar whirring noise.

She spun around and saw that Seth had raised the camera over them, pointed it down, and depressed the button. The little red light was on.

"Seth!" She slapped his chest.

"There! Do you see, Jennifer? Do you see how mean she is to me?"

"Seth, turn that thing off."

"Hi, Jennifer, I'm the guy Summer is sort of, kind of, maybe seeing, part of the time. But she has six other boyfriends, too, although none of them is as *cute* as me."

"They're all cuter," Summer said, laughing. "I'm kidding, Jen, obviously, duh."

"What?" Seth demanded. "Are you saying there are no other guys you're sort of maybe seeing?" He turned off the camera.

Summer started to climb off, but he wouldn't let her go.

"So how much longer do we have to go on avoiding the dreaded B-word?" Seth asked. "You know how I feel about you."

"Seth, we've been all over this at least six times," Summer said. "I just am not going to rush into some big commitment. I'm too young. Besides, what am I supposed to do when summer vacation is over?"

"I guess we'd have to figure that out when the end of summer comes around," Seth said seriously.

"Yeah. You'll be back in Wisconsin with Lianne."

"I'll be back in Wisconsin. Not with Lianne," he said.

Summer shrugged. She got up, crossed the room, and put the camera down on her dresser.

"Can't we not put me under so much pressure?" Summer asked.

Seth sat up on the edge of the bed. "Sure. I'm sorry. I keep saying I won't press you, and then I do it anyway."

"It's not that I don't like you," Summer said. "A lot. I do. I just feel like I'm not ready to get as serious as you want to get."

"You mean, we're not getting married next week? Darn. I'll have to tell my mom the wedding's off."

"Very funny." Summer came back and sat beside him. She took his hand and held it on her lap. "It's . . . I know this is going to sound strange, but I've been thinking a lot lately. I keep having these dreams about my brother."

"Jonathan?"

"Yes. I mean, I think that's what it is. I see this little boy dressed in white. I know, it sounds nuts, I guess, because I never even saw Jonathan. He disappeared months before I was even born. But it's like the idea of him is coming back, and I think maybe it's sort of a warning to me."

"A warning?" Seth looked confused.

Not exactly surprising, Summer realized. This was the first time she'd articulated the feeling that had grown from the mess with Adam and the mess between Marquez and J.T., all combined with Jonathan.

"Look, I know this is silly, but it's like . . . like people forget that loving someone and committing to someone can sometimes be bad. I mean, I think about my parents and Jonathan. It's really messed up their lives in lots of ways, even though they try to not put it off on me."

"Oh." Seth nodded. "I get it."

"You do?"

"Sure," he said. "You think if you get totally into someone you might get hurt."

"Right, so the more slowly you take it and the more totally sure you feel, the less likely it is you'll get hurt."

"That's your theory?"

Summer nodded.

Seth tilted his head back and forth, as if he were holding an internal debate. "I guess I can live with that, for now. Actually, it's kind of nice, in a perverse way. You're saying if you admit you're in love with me and then you lose me, you'll be terribly unhappy."

"You make it sound kind of obvious," Summer said. "It seemed much more profound in my mind."

"The other side of what you're saying is that if we broke up right now, you'd just wash your hands of me, figure no big deal, bring on the next guy." Suddenly he pushed her onto her back and lowered his face to hers. "Too bad, it's not going to work. Because I'm not going to just go away."

He kissed her and for a while, at least, she forgot why it was that she'd ever even thought of losing him.

★   ★   ★

By the next morning, she had remembered.

"Because," she explained to Marquez, who was going through Summer's wardrobe making rude remarks, "the amount of possible pain is directly proportional to the degree of commitment."

"Uh-huh," Marquez said. "Is that geometry? Or algebra?" She held up a bulky sweater of Summer's. "Why is this here? Even in February it doesn't get that cold here. This is July. You have, like, one bathing suit and two sweaters."

"I am trying to discuss an important idea here," Summer said.

"You want an important idea? I'll give you an important idea—what are we doing today? We have the day off."

"I'm going diving with Seth this afternoon," Summer said.

"Okay, so we have the morning off. I repeat, what are we doing? I'm thinking shopping."

"I have nothing to shop for," Summer said.

"You are so wrong. You need so much stuff. And I know you made money Saturday night. You had that ten-top with all the champagne."

There was a knock on the door. "It's me." Diana's voice.

"Come in," Summer yelled.

"Diana," Marquez said. "Out walking in the sunlight? Isn't that dangerous for your species?"

"Ah, Marquez, as always, you're every bit as funny as your taste in outfits," Diana said as she walked to the center of the room.

116

"Ooh, right through the heart," Marquez said. "Diana's been drinking the caffeinated coffee again."

Marquez was right. There had been a noticeable change in Diana lately. She seemed preoccupied and yet jumpy with suppressed energy. Noticeably different from the depressed, sullen Diana Summer had gotten used to.

"I just came down to warn you," Diana said to Summer. "It's finally happening. Mallory is coming home tomorrow. It's definite."

"Oh no," Summer said. "I won't be here tomorrow. I'm going on a diving trip with Seth. We won't get back until late."

"Lucky you," Diana said dryly. She noticed the video camera. "Wait, that's right. You have a video camera, don't you?"

"Yep. Why? Did you want to borrow it?"

"Maybe," Diana said thoughtfully. "Are you taking it on your trip?"

"No, I'd end up getting it wet," Summer said.

"Better and better," Diana said softly.

"What do you mean—" Summer fell silent. The hatchway in the floor had lifted two inches. She peered and saw a pair of eyes she recognized.

"You can come in, Diver, Diana knows about you. She's cool," Summer said. "And you've already met Marquez."

She's cool, Summer thought. Jeez, you sound like you're dealing drugs or something. But it reminded her of the fact that Mallory, Diana's mother, might *not* be so cool, if she learned about Diver.

117

Diver raised the hatch a few inches higher. "Um, hi," he said to Diana. "Nice to meet you and all."

Diana bent over and looked down at him. "I don't know if this is exactly a meeting. But, you know, nice to . . . whatever."

"Come on in," Marquez said with sudden enthusiasm.

"Um, well . . ." Diver said.

He seemed even more at a loss for words than usual. Summer knelt down in front of him. "Is there something wrong?"

"Kind of," Diver said.

"What is it?"

"There was this nail, sticking out of this piling down by the marina, right?" he said.

"A nail. At the marina. Okay."

"See, I was doing this job."

"You work?" Marquez said, surprised. "I thought you just sort of absorbed nutrition from the environment, by osmosis or something."

Diver's eyes tracked left, puzzled. "Osmosis? I believe that's a feature of plants, not animals."

"Diver, what's the problem?" Summer asked impatiently. "Marquez, stop interrupting. Diver, come on in and tell us."

"Well, there was this nail. And I kind of caught my suit on it. And it kind of ripped."

"Ripped? As in——?"

"I was thinking I would just sew it up, right? Only, I don't have a needle or anything. So I was

118

wondering if you had a needle and thread I could use."

"Of course she does," Marquez said enthusiastically. "Climb right on up and we'll fix it for you."

"It's kind of a big rip," Diver said. "I guess the fabric was kind of old and rotten and it just pretty much fell apart."

"All the more reason to come right on up," Marquez said.

"I'll get you a towel to wrap around yourself," Summer said, with a scolding look at Marquez.

"A hand towel," Marquez called after her. "A washcloth."

Moments later Diver emerged into the living room, wearing a large beach towel wrapped around him. He wiggled and shifted until he could safely produce the bathing suit.

Summer held it up for all to see. The fabric was thoroughly rotted. If it hadn't torn, it would have soon disintegrated.

"That's a nasty rip," Marquez said. "All the way from the waistband down. What a shame. Lucky thing Summer gave you that towel." She shot Summer a dirty look.

"I'm glad to meet you, Diver," Diana said, smiling one of her rare smiles.

"Sure," Diver said, looking mightily uncomfortable. He glanced anxiously from Diana to Marquez. He seemed to have a hard time tearing his gaze away from Marquez, who was eyeing him like a hungry lioness sizing up a juicy lamb.

"So . . . where are the rest of your clothes?" Diana asked.

He shrugged. "I had this shirt," he said, looking around vaguely. "I don't remember where I put it, though."

Summer tossed the bathing suit to Diana. "*That* is his entire wardrobe. That and the beach towel he's wearing."

"Huh," Diana said.

"Hmm," Marquez said.

"You guys, try to be mature about this," Summer said. They were grinding her nerves now. The two of them leering and all but drooling. After all, Diver had a brain, and a heart, too. If either Marquez or Diana was interested in him they were going to have to recognize that and treat him with respect.

Good grief, Summer chided herself—what am I, his mother all of a sudden?

"Mature, definitely. Gotta be mature," Marquez agreed.

"Diver, I think maybe you need some new clothes," Summer said.

"I guess so," he agreed. "But how am I going to go and buy them if I'm wearing a towel?"

"Ladies," Marquez announced, rubbing her hands gleefully, "I believe we have found something to do with the rest of the day. We have to buy this boy some clothes. You two get going, and I'll stay here."

"I can put it on Mallory's credit card," Diana

offered. "Might as well do as much damage as I can before she gets back."

"I have money," Diver said.

"You do?" all three girls said at once.

"Sure. I do work, you know. I do stuff like clean boats down at the marina. I have it in a jar, up on the deck. Let me go get it."

He disappeared outside and they heard him climbing up onto the deck.

"Do you realize that he is the best-looking guy on planet earth?" Diana said under her breath. "I mean, I'm not alone in this, am I? He's like . . . He's prettier than any of the three of us. It's not natural."

"Like a perfect specimen," Marquez said dreamily. "This simple, beautiful child of nature, with this beautiful face, and this beautiful body, and just like . . . perfect. Uncomplicated and perfect."

Summer realized she was bridling at their reactions. Not that it would mean anything to Diver. "He isn't interested in girls," Summer whispered. "They disturb his *wa*."

"His *wa*?" Marquez said.

"His *wa*. His inner peace," Diana translated, much to Summer's surprise.

"See what I mean?" Marquez said. "Simple. Uncomplicated. No problems. The perfect guy. Of course, he's going to have to get over this thing about girls. Probably he just hasn't met the right one. What he needs is someone as calm and simple and accepting as he is. Like me."

Summer and Diana both laughed.

"So? I could change," Marquez said, laughing along.

"Oh. No. A terrible thought just occurred to me," Summer said.

"What?"

"We're going to leave Diver here, sitting around in nothing but a towel. Seth is coming over to pick me up. We have to be back before that meeting takes place."

"You had to trust Seth with Lianne, right?" Marquez suggested. "Maybe it's time to see how trusting Seth is. And if he can trust you with Diver . . ." She bit her lip and made a suggestive little movement. "I suppose you have dibs on him, right?" Marquez demanded.

"If she does, then I have dibs on Seth," Diana said. She laughed a little too loudly.

"Dibs?" Summer echoed.

"Dibs. You know, like he's yours or whatever."

"You mean like as a *guy?*" Summer said, incredulous. And what had Diana meant about Seth?

"No, as a pony," Marquez said. "What are you, getting stupid? Of course as a *guy.* I mean, are you going to scratch my eyes out if I happen to, you know, become Mrs. Diver?"

Summer realized she was surprised by the question. She had reacted to Diver a little that way, maybe, right at first. But since then, it hadn't occurred to her. She didn't really think of Diver as a *guy* in the way that Seth was a guy.

"You're taking an awful long time to answer a simple question," Marquez said. "I'm only asking because it would be really excellent to be able to accidentally run into J.T. and Lianne when I was with Diver."

"Sure," Summer said. "I mean, of course, I don't mind. But don't just treat Diver like he's some toy."

"Of course not," Marquez said. "Now, let's get him some clothes and dress him up like a Ken doll."

The girls bought Diver:
    1 pair madras print trunks
    1 Ralph Lauren blue work shirt
    1 pair Levi's 501 jeans
    3 pairs Calvin Klein underwear
    3 pairs white socks
    1 pair Reebok running shoes
    1 Miami Dolphins jersey

In addition, Diana bought herself a large over-the-shoulder bag decorated with gaudy glass beads that everyone agreed was hideous and completely unlike anything Diana would ever be seen carrying in public.

Loaded down with their many gifts, they arrived back at the stilt house to find Seth calmly waiting for Summer. Diver was nowhere in sight. Seth explained that he had given Diver an old pair of extra trunks that he kept in his truck and Diver had taken off.

Marquez then threatened to hurt Seth very badly.

12

The Importance of Being Diver

The marina was downtown, not far from the Crab 'n' Conch. It was a small forest of masts: the tall, elegant masts of sailboats, the stubbier masts of powerboats. Several dozen white-and-blue-hulled boats were arrayed in tight little rows, connected by low wooden piers and adorned here and there with striped awnings, limp flags, flashes of chrome, and deeper tones of weathered teak-wood.

The largest boats were out at the ends of the piers, huge wallowing palaces with uniformed crewmen performing maintenance while tanned women lounged in deck chairs drinking daiquiris. Marquez had stopped at her house to change clothes and try to think up some plausible excuse as to why she should be hanging around the marina. She never went to the marina. The marina was headquarters of the tourists she had to wait on at the restaurant.

She had not yet come up with an excuse. She'd tried out several, all starting with, "Why, Diver, what a surprise to run into *you* here. I was just on my way to . . ."

And that's as far as the excuses went. I was just on my way to . . .

Just on my way to see if you'd like to hang out with me or whatever, because basically I'm trying to get J.T. out of my mind permanently and you seem like just the guy who could make me forget that jerk forever.

"Excellent plan," Marquez muttered under her breath. "Just tell Diver all that and he'll run away, screaming for help."

As it turned out, she had a difficult time finding Diver in the cluttered maze of boats. She had no trouble attracting the attention of several other guys, since she had dressed in a way designed to get attention. But she breezed by them with an air of confident disdain, and they left her alone.

She had reached the end of the main pier and was enjoying a little shade cast by a monstrous cabin cruiser when she heard voices. Feminine voices. She shielded her eyes and saw two women, sunglassed, tanned, liposuctioned, wearing gold-lace sandals and similar black one-piece bathing suits.

They didn't notice her. They were looking in the other direction and talking in low voices.

"Something's different about him," one said.

"Nothing's different. He's still adorable."

"I'm not saying he isn't. I'm just saying, something has changed. I think maybe it's the bathing suit."

"Maybe I'll call him over. We could get him to swab the decks or something."

Marquez had a pretty good idea who they were talking about. And when she went out to the end of the pier she could see Diver, standing up in a tiny dinghy, carefully applying paint to a beautiful, antique sailboat.

She was about to call to him, but then she had a better idea.

Marquez kicked off her sandals and dived into the water. She was halfway to him by the time she surfaced. She took a deep breath and went under again, swimming hard until she could see the little dinghy bobbing overhead.

She surfaced in the narrow space between the dinghy and the side of the sailboat. She spit out a mouthful of seawater, smoothed back her hair, and smiled. "Hi."

He stopped with his paintbrush in midair. "Oh. Hi."

It wasn't exactly giddy enthusiasm she saw on his face.

"I know you, right?" he said.

That nearly wiped the smile off Marquez's face. "Yes, I'm Marquez. You know, Summer's friend." Oh, great. She had to introduce herself as "Summer's friend." Obviously, she'd made a huge impression on him.

"Yeah," he said. He glanced around, looking a bit like a trapped animal.

"Give me a hand," Marquez ordered.

"A hand?"

"Help me up," she said. She stuck a hand up to him.

With reluctance he didn't even try to hide, he took her hand and helped heave her into the dinghy. "Careful, I have paint here. This man who owns the boat is in kind of a hurry."

Marquez sat in the stern of the dinghy and wondered if she wasn't totally wasting her time. She knew perfectly well that she was an attractive girl. An attractive girl wearing a small bathing suit *ought* to have gotten some reaction from Diver—other than the vaguely queasy look he had.

"You're painting the boat, huh?" she said.

"Just this part. See, where it got scraped against a piling."

"Maybe I could help," Marquez said with sudden inspiration. "You know, I paint a lot."

"You do?"

A faint flicker of interest.

"Yes. Some people think I'm a pretty good artist," Marquez said.

"Huh."

"Do you have an extra brush?"

"There." He pointed.

He still looked queasy and ill at ease, but he moved over a little to make room for her to take a

128

brush, dip it, and begin to paint, feathering her edge into his.

"You know, we bought you some clothes. Summer and Diana and me."

"Thanks. This guy let me have this suit, though, so I'm set. This guy named Seth. He's Summer's boyfriend, right?"

What an interesting question, Marquez thought. Why exactly was he asking that? Was Diver interested in Summer? Oh, that would really be a major drag. "Yes, I guess so," Marquez said.

Well, it is the truth—kind of, she told herself. And if it wasn't the complete truth right now, it probably would be soon.

"Huh," Diver commented, a word that told Marquez nothing.

"No doubt you wish I was Summer," Marquez said snippily.

"Why should I? She doesn't paint, does she?"

"Maybe you prefer blondes," Marquez said.

"No, I like dark hair, too," he said.

Marquez told herself not to push it any further, but she never listened to her own advice. "Blue eyes? Is that it? Thighs? You like skinny thighs?"

Diver rested his brush on the lip of the paint can. "I like all kinds of girls," he said seriously. "I just don't do anything about it because they disturb my *wa*. I mean, I guess I'd rather just have a peaceful life."

"Uh-huh. So, do *I* disturb your *wa*?"

"Yes, very much," he said.

"Excellent," Marquez said, beaming with self-satisfaction. For the next thirty minutes, much to Marquez's frustration, Diver said not a word. She decided she should not force herself on him, so she remained silent, too. After all, she admired his strangeness, so she shouldn't be annoyed by it.

When they'd finished painting he looked at her, quickly looked away, and said, "Thanks. I can give you some of the money the guy is paying me."

"No, no," Marquez said with a laugh. "I didn't do it for money."

"Oh. Why did you do it?"

Good question, Marquez realized. Her bathing suit now had two speckles of white paint. And she had learned exactly nothing new about Diver.

"Like I said, I enjoy painting," she said.

"Cool."

"Um, in fact, I'd really . . . I mean, it would be cool if you would come over and take a look at my paintings. *At* my house, I mean." Marquez held her breath. This would be the point at which he would live out the meaning of his name and dive over the side of the boat, never to return.

"I guess I could," he said.

Marquez was delighted. And surprised. "Let's go, then," she said. Show him her paintings. Maybe they could share a little snack. Then, with any luck at all, she could begin to convince him that it wasn't such a bad thing to have your *wa* disturbed.

*　　*　　*

"This is my tree," Marquez said with a flourish of her hand. "See. The roots go out across the floor, then the trunk goes all the way up the wall, and the branches and leaves spread out across the ceiling."

Diver tilted back his head to take it all in. He nodded solemnly.

Marquez was a bit nonplussed by his reaction. The tree was her best thing. She pointed out several other features of her walls. "That's the moon, of course, and the sun." Yeah, like he wouldn't recognize the moon or the sun. "The moon and the stars are painted with fluorescent colors, so that way, when you turn off the lights at night, they keep glowing for a while. Want to see?"

She flipped off the lights, plunging the room into almost total darkness. The sprinkling of stars on the ceiling glowed an eerie white. Then she turned the lights back on.

Diver seemed to guess that some response was being called for. "Cool," he said. He turned and focused on the graffiti names that intertwined with the many other small paintings. He pointed to a patch of pure white. "What's this?"

Marquez sighed. Perfect. He'd focused on the one thing she really did not want to discuss. "That's just something I wanted to cover over," she said.

"A name?"

"Yes, a name. Some guy's name." J.T., to be exact. She had covered it with three coats of white. And still she had the feeling she could make out the letters beneath.

"Did he die?"

"Die? No. Why would he be dead?"

"You erased him."

"Look, it's just some guy I didn't want to re-member anymore."

Diver nodded. He remained focused with sin-gular intensity on the painted-out J.T.

"I think it's good to remember things," Diver said softly.

"Some things yes, some things no," Marquez said impatiently.

"I don't think you can choose that way. I think you either remember stuff or you don't. It's not like you can just erase things. I mean, not deliberately, anyway."

Marquez had the distinct sense that Diver was telling her something important, but at the same time she was feeling harassed and annoyed. She had Diver right here in her room, and all they could talk about was J.T. Or the lack of J.T.

"Diver, J.T. is just my ex-boyfriend, okay? Things got strange between us, or at least *he* got strange, and now that's over."

He nodded. Then he smiled impishly. "I guess I should be careful not to get strange, huh?"

Now what exactly did that mean? "You want to listen to some music?" Marquez asked. No answer. He had moved on now, reading each name on her wall as if he was trying to memorize them.

Marquez chose a CD and hit Play. The music was danceable without being too loud. The plan was to see if Diver liked to dance. So far he had failed one of her tests of a worthy human being—he had not exactly been enthusiastic about her painting. But if he could dance, he might make up for that.

Marquez let the music seep through her, let it touch the control buttons in her mind that started her body swaying in time to the rhythm.

"I don't see Summer," Diver said.

"I'll put her up soon," Marquez said. "I haven't decided on the letters or the color yet. I'm thinking gold and blue."

Diver actually smiled. "Yes, gold and blue. Those are her colors."

"And what colors am I?" Marquez asked playfully.

Diver looked at her thoughtfully, concentrating, as if she had asked him a perfectly serious question. "You're like sunrise or sunset. Red and yellow and orange, fading into purple. Bright, intense colors. If they lasted too long they'd be overwhelming and make everything else look pale. So they just appear for a short time and then fade away, and you're wondering if they were even real. And then they reappear, but never for so long that you get tired of them. Just a short glimpse, and that's all you need."

Marquez swallowed hard. Okay, she was willing to forgive his lack of interest in her walls. She stepped closer. He did not run away.

He did not become any less attractive up close.

"Um, would you like to dance?" she asked him.

"I don't dance very much," he said.

That was it. He'd failed both her tests. Too bad she just didn't care.

"Can I ask you something, Diver?"

"If you want."

"Is Diver your real name?"

His crystal–clear eyes seemed to cloud over. "I don't think so," he said.

"What do you mean, you don't think so?" Marquez said, smiling.

"Never mind. I guess either way, I'm me," he said simply. "I have to go."

"What are you talking about?" Marquez demanded. "You just got here. And don't start talking about your *wa* again."

He laughed self-deprecatingly. "Okay, I won't. But I still have to go."

Marquez threw up her hands. "What is it with me and guys? Do you know why I brought you here?"

"To show me your painting?"

"No, no, no. Because you were supposed to become interested in me. You were going to really like my paintings, and then we would maybe dance, and then, I figured unless I have totally lost it, you'd kiss me and I'd kiss you, and I'd tell you it was something I'd been wanting to do ever since I saw you."

"Oh."

Suddenly the telephone began to ring.

Diver stepped closer, and then, without warning, kissed Marquez lightly on the lips.

He drew back. "Did that make you happy?" he asked.

Marquez just groaned.

"I have to go now," Diver said for the third time.

The telephone rang again.

"Well, bye then," Marquez said.

He walked away, leaving her feeling as far from happy as she had felt in a long time.

The phone rang yet again.

Marquez snatched up the receiver. "YES, YES, YES, YES, what the hell is it and it had better be good!" She listened for a moment. "Sure," she said in a slightly more subdued voice. "Sure. I'd love to come to work. Why not? I obviously have no life!"

13

Shoot-out at the Cramp 'n' Croak

What are you doing here?" Summer demanded.

"What do you mean, what am I doing here? They called me in to hostess," Marquez said. "What are you two doing here?"

The Crab 'n' Conch was half-full with early-dining families, old people just finishing up, and the first few later-dining couples being seated.

"We are celebrating," Seth said. He stood behind Summer, took her hands, and spread her arms out in a "ta-daa!" position. "You are looking at a certified scuba diver. As of about an hour ago. Take a bow, Summer."

Summer took a little bow, which Seth did along with her. "Seth is buying me dinner, so we would like a window table."

"Oh, you'd like a window table, huh? You think you get special treatment?" Marquez asked.

"You know," Summer said, batting her eyes, "you look great in that dress. I mean it. Like a model. I wish I had your body and your hair."

Marquez laughed. "You're going to need your scuba gear to breathe in here if the crap gets piled any deeper. Okay, okay, I'll get you a window table." She grabbed a couple of menus. "At least *someone* thinks I look good, even if it is just another girl."

"What are you talking about, Marquez?" Summer asked.

Marquez stopped, handed the menus to Seth, and pointed to an empty table. "Here, take these and go seat yourself. I have to talk to Summer."

"Oh, fine," Seth grumbled. "Just dump the guy."

Marquez took Summer's arm and drew her away to a corner of the coatroom. "Don't get mad or anything, all right?" Marquez said. "I had Diver over at my house."

"Why would I be mad?" Summer said in a phony, shrill voice. "It's none of my business."

"Uh-huh. Anyway, it didn't work out all that great."

"Oh, really?"

"Don't gloat," Marquez said. "It just turned out . . . I don't know. It's like there's more going on with him than I thought. Also less. I mean, I think he may have problems."

"Like what?"

"Like he doesn't *know* his own name. Either he doesn't remember, like he has amnesia or something, or else he was just blowing me off."

"Puh-leeze, he was just blowing you off. That's the way he always is. You can never get a straight answer out of Diver. Diver's . . . I don't know. He's just Diver. But of course *you* had to cross-examine him."

"I asked a couple of simple questions," Marquez said.

"And now you don't like the answers."

"I thought I would like the answers," Marquez said crossly. "I guess."

"Maybe you shouldn't have asked questions. I thought you liked him because he was so simple and innocent and not at all like J.T. And then you start in on him?"

"I didn't 'start in on him.' I was trying to get something going, that's all. Just because you treat him like your platonic guy friend, doesn't mean *I* have to," Marquez grumbled. "Maybe *you* don't notice how he looks anymore, but I do."

Summer felt troubled. "I'd hate to think he actually has amnesia or something. That means he's sick, kind of."

"Yeah. Besides, what happens if he regains his memory and it turns out he's really some kind of preppy weasel who buys all his clothes out of the J. Crew catalog? Then what?"

"Excuse me, *this* is from J. Crew," Summer said, pointing to her blouse.

The manager of the restaurant stuck his head around the corner. "Oh, *there* you are, Marquez. Maybe I should just tell the customers who are waiting at the hostess stand to come find you back here."

"I'm on my way," Marquez promised. Then, to Summer in an undertone, "I volunteer to work an extra shift and he's ragging on me anyway."

"You'd better go," Summer said. "We'll talk later. Maybe we can figure out if Diver needs some kind of help. Maybe *we* could help him." She smiled wryly. "Help him turn into a preppy weasel."

Marquez rolled her eyes. "Oh, great. Look, if I wanted to be Mother Teresa and help screwed-up guys I'd help J.T. He was first in line."

"You know, this really is a nice view," Summer said, gazing out through the floor-to-ceiling windows as she smoothed the cloth napkin on her lap. "I work here, but it's like I never have time to really notice it."

Outside was the dock, congested with evening strollers enjoying the early stages of sunset and the slight relief from the heat. It was the usual collection of humanity as it appeared on Crab Claw Key—too-fat people showing too much skin, too-fair tourists with bright red sunburns, too-rich people with too little taste.

But there were families as well, pushing baby strollers and trailing bright helium balloons; young married couples on their honeymoons, looking glazed and tired and ostentatiously sharing ice cream cones; then, like a time-lapse photograph, the older couples, gray men and bottle-blond women wearing gaudy matching outfits and sharing secret smiles and knowing winks with their partners as they watched their younger selves pass by.

"I should pay more attention to things," Summer said thoughtfully. "There's a lot going on."

Seth looked up from his menu and followed the direction of her gaze. "Kind of a good show, isn't it?" he said. "I mean, I don't know what Bloomington, Minnesota, is like, but where I'm from, in Eau Claire, you don't usually see this many different kinds of people."

"I suppose Eau Claire and Bloomington aren't very different," Summer said. "More like each other than either of them is like Crab Claw Key. Not that people there are boring or all the same— they aren't. But everything here is raised to a more extreme level."

"That's good *and* bad, I guess," Seth said.

"I know. You have to watch out or you lose yourself here, right?" She gave Seth an affectionate smile. "I remember you telling me that. What was it? 'Tropical rot'?"

Seth laughed. "Did I say that? Hmm, sounds like me, I have to admit." He grew more serious. "I think that at the time I just wanted to find some way to keep you from falling for Adam Merrick."

Summer's smile faded. "I guess I'd have been better off if I'd listened to you."

Seth kept his face immobile, but in his eyes

there was a smug, satisfied look that annoyed Summer just a little.

"Go ahead. You want to say 'I told you so,'" Summer said.

"No, I don't," Seth said. "I don't want you to feel bad. I just want—"

"Yo, Summer, what are you doing in here? Trying to pretend you're a tourist?"

They both looked up and saw J.T., wearing his usual cook's whites. But there was something different, Summer realized—for once, his apron was clean.

J.T. noticed her dubious stare. "I can't come out into the dining room looking like my usual disaster area," he explained. "Seth, right?" He held out his hand to Seth.

Seth shook it. "Yeah, we met once, I guess, back last year when you and Marquez were . . . Um . . . Well, I stepped right in it, didn't I?"

J.T. waved it off. "Forget it, man. Ancient history. I just came out to see if I can cook up something special for my favorite waitress."

Just then Lianne walked up to the table, her order pad at the ready.

"I thought *I* was your favorite waitress, J.T.," she said, looking up at him with a look of near-adoration.

J.T. returned the intimate smile. "Well . . ."

Lianne looked coolly down at Seth and deliberately put her arm around J.T.'s waist. J.T. put his arm around Lianne.

Seth looked at Lianne. Then he looked at J.T. He was clearly trying not to react, but Lianne had been his girlfriend for years.

Lianne shot a triumphant look at Summer. A look that said, "See, you may have Seth now, but I'm not exactly crying myself to sleep every night." Then Lianne turned a slow, cold smile on Seth.

J.T. glanced sheepishly at Summer, suffering the usual male embarrassment at any public display of affection. But he had forgotten the more important point—Seth was Lianne's former boyfriend. Then, seeming to make the connection in his mind, his eyes widened and he looked a bit nervously at Seth.

Just to complete the circle of discomfort, Marquez sauntered up.

Marquez instantly spotted Lianne's arm around J.T.'s waist. Her nostrils flared. Her lip tried to jerk itself into a sneer.

J.T. shifted uncomfortably, as though he suddenly wished Lianne's arm was somewhere else. Or at least wished *he* was somewhere else.

Seth took a deep breath and prudently buried his face in his menu.

Marquez sent Lianne a look that could have frozen the sun. But Lianne returned the look with one of defiant spite.

"So," Summer said brightly. "What's good on the menu tonight?" This was dangerous. Diver had just blown off Marquez. This was not the time for her to be around J.T. and Lianne acting lovey-dovey.

"Maybe you should get back in the kitchen," Marquez said to J.T. "Cooks aren't supposed to be out here making the place look bad."

"What are you, the manager now?" J.T. shot back.

"How about if *you* go back to the hostess stand," Lianne said to Marquez. "This is *my* table. I'm their waitress. It's my responsibility."

Summer saw the flame light up in Marquez's eyes. "Marquez, let's all just—" Summer began. Too late.

"Then why don't you *act* responsible instead of hanging all over the cook, practically feeling him up here in the middle of the restaurant. People are trying to eat."

Lianne sucked in her breath sharply. "How is this *any* of your business, Marquez? You and J.T. are not together anymore. So get lost."

"Only a sleazy lowlife would go after some guy who just broke up with his girlfriend," Marquez said in a voice that carried clearly to several adjoining tables. "I mean, are you so desperate you're going to jump all over J.T. when he and I just broke up a few weeks ago?"

Lianne lowered her voice to a silky, dangerous tone. "Is that so, Marquez. Then what about your friend Summer?"

Marquez looked blank. "What?"

"You may notice she's here with Seth, even though Seth and I just broke up. If I'm a sleazy lowlife, then so is Summer."

"That's different," Marquez said lamely. She sent Summer a quick shrug of apology.

"Lianne, why don't you just leave me and Summer out of this," Seth said quietly, emerging from his menu.

"Oh, perfect. Sethie doing his protective thing, as always," Lianne sneered. "Sethie is so protective. Like an extra father."

Summer glanced at Seth. He looked angry but calm. She felt embarrassed. It was pretty clear that J.T. felt the same way. Their eyes met. He shrugged helplessly.

"Look, how about if we—"

"Look, how about if we—"

Summer stopped and looked at J.T. in confusion. They had both said the same thing at the same moment.

"I was just going to say, how about if we all back off and start over again," J.T. said.

Summer nodded in agreement. "Yeah. Let's stop all this, okay, guys?" Her gaze met J.T.'s again. She saw her own troubled feelings reflected in his eyes.

To Summer's surprise, Marquez was suddenly reasonable. "Summer's right. Let's try and act our ages." To J.T. she added, "As opposed to our IQs." And to Lianne, "Or our bra size."

Well, as reasonable as Marquez ever was.

J.T. looked sheepish. "How about if I just go back to my kitchen and Marquez goes back to the hostess stand, and, um, maybe we'll just get someone else besides Lianne to wait on you."

"Whatever you say, sweetheart," Lianne said to J.T., adding extra emphasis to the *sweetheart*. "I'll ask Tony to come over."

When they were all gone, Summer and Seth looked at each other for a few seconds in complete silence.

It was Summer who cracked first. She grinned. "See? This kind of stuff never used to happen back in Bloomington."

Seth chuckled. "Not in Eau Claire, either."

"It's that tropical rot," Summer said. She began to giggle. "I think we should run for it."

"Right behind you. I know a place where we can get some conch fritters. And then tomorrow we'll spend the whole day underwater with nice, sensible fish."

Marquez waited for an hour before she got the opportunity to corner J.T. She lurked around until she saw him go into the walk-in refrigerator. She glanced behind her, making sure that Lianne was nowhere in sight, then she swiftly followed him in. He had his back turned to her as he counted portions of fish in long steel trays.

She wasted no time on preliminaries. "I can't believe you would replace me with that skinny little witch Lianne. I thought you had better taste than that."

"Go away, Marquez. I have work to do."

"You totally made a fool of yourself out there," Marquez said. "I hope you're satisfied."

J.T. turned around. "I don't get it, Marquez. What do you want from me?"

"Nothing. I don't want anything from you," she said.

"Yeah? Then why are you here?"

"I just wanted to tell you I can't believe you're seeing Lianne."

"Why is it any of your business?"

"I have a right to have an opinion," Marquez said. "And that's my opinion. It's a free country."

J.T. sighed. "What is it with you? You dump me, but then you can't handle it when I start seeing someone else? What's that about?"

"Like I said, I can't believe you're going with Lianne, that's all. She's only the witch of the universe. You know what she did to try to hang on to Seth? Did you hear about that? How she tried to make Summer think she was sleeping with Seth? That's the kind of girl you want to go out with?"

To Marquez's surprise, J.T. nodded. "Yes," he said with perfect seriousness. "Maybe it is. So she went too far, trying to hold on to a relationship she cared about. At least she *did* care. At least she tried. Unlike some people who walk away as soon as things get a little difficult. Maybe that seems like a pretty good thing to me, right now. I'd like to know what it's like to have a girlfriend who cared enough to fight for me."

The remark stung Marquez, and she struck back, harder than she'd intended. "Did you tell her all about your little fantasy that your parents aren't your real parents? Did you tell her all about how nuts you went?"

"Yes, I did," J.T. said softly. "I told her all of it. I told her it made me feel lost and confused. That I loved my parents, but I was worried about what it meant that I didn't have a birth certificate or adoption papers."

"You *told* her?"

"Yeah. And you know what? She didn't run for the nearest exit. Unlike certain people. She didn't just blow me off and tell me to get over it. Unlike certain people."

Marquez could tell him, tell him right now what she suspected about him and Summer and a lost boy named Jonathan. It would probably devastate him. He would be upset. He would feel hurt. Maybe it would serve him right. At this moment, she wanted to hurt him.

And then he would run straight to Lianne, and Lianne would comfort him.

"I'm sure it was a very sweet, tender scene," Marquez said, sneering as contemptuously as she could manage. But it wasn't very convincing. She suddenly realized she felt an ache inside her chest. She felt hollow. Empty. The cold of the walk-in seemed very noticeable.

J.T. wasn't just seeing Lianne to spite Marquez. That was a new and disturbing realization.

"It was something new for me," J.T. said. "I felt bad, and she made me feel better. And she told me how bad she felt over Seth, and I guess I made *her* feel better. I understand that's what relationships are like."

"But you're not . . . serious or anything," Marquez said. "Not about *Lianne?*"

He shook his head, almost pityingly. "I have work to do."

14

I don't really have much time to do this, Jen, but I wanted to get in one last message before I mail this off. I just played back the part of the tape with Seth and me on it. He's usually more serious than he was being there.

Tomorrow morning Seth and I are going on a diving trip, now that I'm an official scuba diver, over to this island called Geiger Key. No one lives there, but the diving is supposed to be really cool. They have a sunken freighter and all these caves that are full of fish and stuff, and Seth says the tourists don't go there much.

Listen to me—like *I'm* some kind of local.

Anyway, it's going to be like an all-day thing. We won't get back until late. He kind of suggested we could just camp out overnight, but I gave that a big N-O. Last time I stayed overnight somewhere was at Adam's. Besides, if I said yes, Seth would just think it was a sign I was ready to make some big commitment, which I'm not.

I don't even know why, Jen, it's just this feeling I've had. I keep having the same dreams about Jonathan. I don't know why. I never, ever used to dream about him. I think maybe it's some kind of warning, you know, about losing someone you love. What else could it be?

Okay, yes, I know, it could be that I'm just having dreams and no big deal. Or else I'm eating pizza before I go to bed and it's giving me nightmares. Only they aren't nightmares. They're tied up somehow with being down here. I don't know, forget it, I'm babbling.

I have no time to babble. I have to get ready for this trip tomorrow. I'm really looking forward to it.

At least, I think I am. I really love diving now. And I really like spending time with Seth. Maybe that's the problem: I like spending time with him too much. Oh well, things could be worse.

And look, look at this—tan line. Definite tan line. That puts my Florida tan ahead of your California tan, I believe. Anyway . . . I have to get to bed early, be rested and all. Long day tomorrow. And I'm really looking forward to it.

What I'm not looking forward to is falling asleep tonight and having that dream again.

15

Getting In Deeper and Deeper

*I*t was a two-hour trip by boat, flying along over the light chop, skipping from wave to wave almost as fast as by car. Ten minutes into the trip Summer had felt a little seasick from the constant up-and-down movement, the series of small and large shocks, but then, after a while, her body adjusted. She managed not to hurl, which she considered a major accomplishment.

Seth had borrowed the boat from a friend. It was not as sleek as Adam's boat, but it felt safe enough and was as fast as Summer could stand.

The morning had started gray and overcast with fog that had hidden the sun and turned the water dark and threatening. But by nine in the morning the fog had burned away, and soon after, the clouds blew away to the west. Now, as they neared the small, low island, the sun was at full midmorning intensity, climbing the blue sky, turning the water green and translucent, like an antique glass bottle.

"There it is, Geiger Key," Seth yelled over the roar of the engines. "Either that or I've gone too far and it's Cuba. In which case we can go visit Marquez's relatives." He throttled down, reducing speed.

"I don't see any other boats," Summer said, scanning with a hand over her eyes to block the sun. The island was little more than a stretch of beach some quarter-mile long, a boomerang-shaped sandbar with a decorative fringe of palm trees and some low bushes clumped around incongruous outcroppings of rock. It looked as if a few good waves could wash it away permanently. "Not much to it, is there?" Summer said. "I mean, somehow you expect to see some waterfront condos or a Marriott."

"It's not what's above the water that counts, it's what's down below," Seth said. He reduced speed still further, letting the boat creep along the shoreline, close enough to the beach so that Summer could have easily swum ashore. The sand was pure white and smooth—no human foot-prints, no tire tracks, just the tiny three-toed prints of shore birds.

A dozen or so tiny sanderlings scurried busily along the wet sand, evading the lapping edge of the surf. A snow-white egret stood nearby, looking superior and a little stupid on its tall, toothpick legs.

"How do you know when we're in the right spot?" Summer wondered.

"See that big palm there? And that rocky out-cropping there? I just line them up. Nothing to it, once you know where to look."

Seth looked confident, but the isolation of the little island, in the middle of what looked like a million square miles of trackless Gulf water, was a little intimidating to Summer. They hadn't seen another boat in the last half hour. And with the constant roar of the boat's engines suddenly gone, it seemed to Summer that the world was vast and empty around them. Endless blue sky above, broken only by a few cotton ball clouds far off, the endless blue-green sea around them, and nothing to cling to in all that emptiness but this minuscule boat and a scarcely larger island.

"Quiet, isn't it?" Seth whispered, grinning, as if he'd read her mind.

"It does kind of make you want to whisper, like being in a huge museum or church or something."

"So, ready to suit up?" He climbed up onto the bow, freed the anchor, and threw it over the side.

"I guess so," Summer said, still oppressed by the isolation. "Okay, we have to pace ourselves, stay down a little while, then take a break before we go down again. I thought maybe we'd have a picnic lunch on the beach after we work up an appetite. Eat those sandwiches you made."

"Cool," Summer said, trying to sound as non-chalant as he.

Since her first dive, Summer had grown competent at the ritual of suiting up—sliding into the tight rubber jacket, adjusting it to eliminate uncomfortable binding, carefully seating the straps of her tank, automatically checking her air hose and regulator, even spitting into her face mask like a professional.

Seth double-checked every step, watching over her protectively.

"Ready?" he asked.

"Ready."

"Okay, now remember, keep clear of any sharp edges. There's rusted steel down there, and you don't want to slice your air hose. If you do and I'm right there, we'll buddy breathe, right? Otherwise, make an ascent with the air you have. Just remember—"

"Never rise faster than the smallest bubble," Summer said. "I'll be good."

"And of course, look out for old Stinker," Seth said.

"Who— what—?"

"Oh, he's the great white shark who hangs around here. Huge." Seth spread his hands as far as they would go. "He's got a mouth wider than this. They say he got fat on the bodies of all the guys who went down with the freighter, and he's never lost his taste for human flesh."

Summer turned pale.

"I'm kidding," Seth said, terribly amused by his joke. "Kidding. Just a little diving humor."

To show him he hadn't scared her, Summer calmly sat down on the side of the boat, pulled down her mask, and rolled backward into the sea. Once under, she took a quick survey, just in case Seth hadn't really been joking. There were no sharks, as far as she could see.

There was a depth-charge explosion as Seth dropped into the water above her. He paddled down and took a slow inspection tour around her, checking her gear one more time. Then, with a "follow me" wave, he was off.

Summer twisted to point in the same direction, then gave several hard kicks to catch up.

Suddenly, out of nowhere, a blizzard swirled around her, a tornado of tiny silver-and-black fish that sparkled like diamonds in the flickering shafts of sunlight and blocked her view of Seth. In her various practice dives, Summer had never seen more than a few distant fish and, once, a graceful stingray. Now it was if she had been invited to join the school of fish as it darted left and right, seemingly all of one mind, then shot forward, following some unknowable logic.

Just as suddenly as it had come, the blizzard of fish blew away and there was Seth, wiggling his eyebrows, an expression that Summer translated as "wasn't that cool?" She nodded.

The wreck of the freighter was scarcely recognizable at first. It looked more like a natural phenomenon, a rusted, shell-encrusted, half-buried reef shaggily adorned with waving seaweed.

But as they got closer, Summer could see the distinctive outlines of a large ship lying on its side, the superstructure mostly buried, the hull still rising from the sea bed.

It was this strange, out-of-place work of man that made Summer feel most alien. She was flying far above it, hovering over it like an ungainly, slow-motion bird. She felt a passing moment of giddiness, a fear of heights, as if she might at any moment lose the buoyancy of the water and fall the twenty or thirty feet to the dead ship.

Seth led the way down, gliding through the separate beams of milky sunlight, one moment dark, the next bright. Summer kept close to him, oppressed by the sense of distant tragedy. Had people died here, going down with this ship?

Summer and Seth skimmed above the ship's crusty flank, inches above the hull, like airplanes buzzing a landing field. She touched the ship, surprised at the sensation—it was hard and real and substantial. She glanced ahead and saw that Seth was standing upright, using his hands to keep his balance. He waved for her to come.

He was standing beside a huge, jagged tear in the ship's side. The death wound, Summer had no doubt. She looked down into the darkness of the ship. And then, from the dark gash a pop-eyed face appeared, a large fish that looked for all the world like a grumpy old man who'd been awakened from his nap. It floated out and past them, nearly three feet long and in no hurry at all.

Summer gazed around more closely, looking less at the wreck of the ship and more at all the living things on or around or within it. Tiny shells clustered on the hull, each a living creature; the octopus that scuttled along, a liquid flurry of graceful motion; the amazing snail that crept toward her foot. There were small forests of soft, willowy plants that made a home for crabs and squid and rays. Fish, big and small, alone or in schools, darted in and out, up and down, crossing between her and the sun above like flights of birds.

In a single moment of awareness she realized that the dead ship was no longer dead. The machine that had failed to protect its human cargo now protected an entire universe of colorful, indescribably strange, stunningly creative, incredible life.

A moment ago she had been sad, seeing only a wreck. Now she smiled—as well as she could with a regulator in her mouth—and felt a surge of happiness. It was a new, unexpected sort of happiness, a satisfied feeling that had nothing directly to do with her own wants and desires. It was funny, really, Summer thought, the way she got caught up in her own minuscule fears and worries, her own tiny plans, as if she were the star in the big story of the universe.

Just like the people on this ship who had probably

seen nothing but tragedy when it sank, perhaps the confirmation of their own minuscule fears and the end of their own tiny plans. Those people had not been the whole story, either. A much bigger story was being told.

Summer laughed an explosion of bubbles. And then, for some reason that she could not possibly have explained in words, she swam over to Seth. She caught his hands in hers and drew him into a swirling, giddy dance that went round and round and round, a slow tornado of bubbles and limbs caught in a shaft of sunlight.

"So aren't you going to ask me about the trip?" Mallory Olan demanded. She was in the passenger seat of the Mercedes, having said she was just too exhausted to drive after the overnight flight in from the West Coast.

Mallory looked almost nothing like her daughter. She was expensively, if loudly, dressed. Her hair was big and out of a bottle. It was flattened a little in back from leaning against the airline seat.

Diana hated to drive with her mother in the car. It wasn't that her mother criticized her driving; she rarely did. Rather it was that Diana had to cope with morbid fantasies of running the car into a concrete abutment and killing her mother. It wasn't exactly a wish, and it wasn't exactly a fear. But it was distracting.

"How was your trip?" Diana asked.

Mallory began to tell her, in great detail, and

after a few minutes Diana forgot her mother was talking. This day was not even supposed to come. At one point Diana had nearly decided that she would be dead on the day her mother returned. She'd played that scene so many times in her mind that it seemed unreal that her mother should now be here, right beside her, chattering away and complaining, and Diana, far from being dead, was being forced to interject semi-interested "uh-huh's" and "hmm's."

Well, maybe that wasn't *so* far from being dead.

Diana popped in a CD. Butthole Surfers. She didn't especially like them. She only had the CD in the car so that when her mother tried to be "cool" and ask about the band, she could tell Mallory their name and watch her mouth pucker.

"I can't wait to see Summer," Mallory said, shouting over the anarchic music. "I feel bad that I haven't even seen her for more than a minute since she's been here. What *is* this music? They're just screaming."

"It's a tender love song," Diana said, straight-faced.

"Why didn't Summer come with you to pick me up?"

Diana enjoyed the moment. "Summer is off with a boy she met. I guess they're going to spend the day scuba diving and nude sunbathing on an uninhabited island. Don't worry, though. I made sure they packed plenty of sunblock."

161

Okay, so the part about nude sunbathing had been a slight embellishment. And who cared about the sunblock.

Unfortunately, Mallory didn't fall for it. "I'm glad she's meeting people," she said.

They arrived at the house, and the housekeeper came out to help with the bags. The phone was ringing as they went inside.

Her mother grabbed it in the hallway, assuming of course it was for her. And it almost certainly was, Diana thought. She was dragging one bag down the hall when she heard her mother say, "Adam! How nice to hear from you. It's been a long time."

Diana dropped the bag.

"Yes, I had a fine trip," Mallory said. "Me, too. Yes, here's Diana now." She put her hand over the receiver and in a loud stage whisper called Diana over. "It's Adam Merrick." Then she wiggled her eyebrows suggestively.

Diana took the receiver. Her heart rate had shot up as soon as she'd heard the name Adam.

"Yes?"

His voice was curt, cold, formal. "You wanted a meeting. My father is in town today. Four o'clock this afternoon, at the estate. That is, if you're still sure you want this."

He sounded as if he expected her to argue or perhaps to have changed her mind.

"You and Ross, too," she said. She glanced at her mother, who was looking expectant, as if somehow Diana might be discussing marriage plans with Adam.

"Oh, we'll be there," Adam sneered.

Diana hung up the phone.

"So? So, has something been happening while I was away?" Mallory asked.

To Diana's own amazement, she laughed. Well, it *was* funny. "All sorts of things have happened while you were away," Diana said.

16

Seth Crosses the Line, and Adam Crosses Back Over It.

*I*f it wasn't for that beer can, you would almost think no other person had ever been here before," Summer said, gazing down the beach.

The boat bobbed contentedly just offshore, pulling at its anchor rope. They had brought their blanket and picnic supplies ashore in a tiny inflatable dinghy, after exhaling themselves into a giddy high inflating it. The dinghy was just large enough for their things, with the two of them swimming alongside. Now it sat on the sand, limp and partly deflated.

They had laid out their blanket under the shade of a stand of palms, enjoying their peanut butter and jelly and sliced turkey sandwiches while they watched pelicans dive-bombing the water.

For the most part, they'd been silent. It didn't bother Summer. She'd noticed that this easy silence often fell over them after they went for a dive. As if they were reluctant to reintegrate into the normal world of conversations that were carried on in words rather than gestures.

Summer stood up, brushing sand off the seat of her bathing suit, and walked up the beach to pry the can out of the wet sand. When she looked back she saw that Seth was bent over, collecting the debris of their picnic and putting it all in a plastic bag. She started back, then paused for a moment, unnoticed by Seth, enjoying the scene. Seth had the gift of seeming perfectly at home in every environment—when he was hammering and sawing and covered with sweat and sawdust; when he was sitting down to a dinner in a nice restaurant wearing the infrequent shirt; when he was underwater in a wet suit or just a bathing suit. She supposed it was something that came from inside him, this easiness in his own skin, the understated confidence. Not showy or charismatic like Adam, just centered and calm and sure of himself.

Even when he was holding her in his arms, looking solemn and serious, even as he . . .

Especially then, Summer realized with a pleasurable twinge. She walked back to him, and he held the bag open for her can. She bent to pick up a sandy crust of peanut butter and jelly sandwich that had fallen.

Summer wiped her sticky fingers on Seth's bare, smooth chest.

"Hey," he protested.

"Sorry, I forgot to bring paper towels," she said.

"And that's all I am to you—a paper towel." He grabbed her and swung her to the ground. In contrast to the roughness with which he'd grabbed her, he kissed her with supreme gentleness, on her forehead, on her closed eyelids, on her throat, on her left ear . . . on her lips.

His lips were salty, as Summer supposed she was, herself. Salty and no longer so gentle. He kissed her deeply. Summer wrapped her arms around his neck and pulled him closer still, suddenly possessed by a hunger that the peanut butter and jelly sandwiches hadn't exactly addressed. Summer smoothed her own hands down his sunwarmed back, savoring the heat of his skin. Seth pulled his lips away, but only to kiss her neck, and then to move in slow, ever-so-slow increments toward the first swell of her breast.

"Um, wait," Summer said, quite suddenly.

Seth raised his head and smiled. "Did I cross the 'line of death'?"

Summer laughed and kissed him again, but in a way that signaled that they were done—for now. "I don't know if it's exactly a 'line of death.'"

"But it *is* a line," he said.

"Um, yes. I don't exactly know where it's located," she said, "but I know when you've reached it."

"Is it"—he touched the swell of her breast where it met the edge of her bathing suit—"there?"

"Mmm, could be," she said. "But it's more like in my head."

"Oh, *that* line," he said thoughtfully. "You mean the line where you suddenly realize you aren't exactly thinking clearly anymore and something *else* is taking over?"

"So you know that line?" Summer said, trying to make a joke out of it.

He nodded. "I go there every time I'm with you," he said seriously. "I've been living right on that line since the first time I kissed you in the airport."

Summer unintentionally made a little whimpering noise deep in her throat. "Sure. Right. You probably went to the line with lots of girls. Like you never did with Lianne?"

"Did you with Adam?"

Yes, she had, Summer realized. On a night that had a certain similarity with this day. There had been a beach. There had been a picnic. It had seemed a perfect day up to that point. And then . . .

"I think we should go back in the water," Summer said, pushing him back but not urgently.

"She says, avoiding the question."

"I just think we both might cool off a little in the water," Summer said. She got to her feet and helped drag a reluctant Seth to his.

"The water's warm. We'd have to go deep to cool off," he said. "And you are trying so hard to stay shallow." He paused for a beat, then grinned unexpectedly.

Summer began to giggle.

"Okay, that did sound a little pretentious and serious, even for me," Seth said. "Come on, let's get wet."

Diana dressed carefully, almost as if she were performing a ritual. She combed her hair. She brushed her teeth. She checked the tape recorder batteries and the tape itself. She slipped the tape recorder into the waistband of her loose-fitting silk slacks and carefully fluffed the tail of her blouse, checking the result in her mirror.

She had checked it all a dozen times, hundreds, if you counted just running the plan over and over in her mind. The small tape recorder could not be seen or heard. She had taped over the little red indicator light after an early experiment had revealed that it shined through.

Diana picked up the bag she'd bought. It was a hideous thing. Fortunately, neither Adam nor Ross had ever had much fashion sense when it came to female styles.

Diana went downstairs, sidling past the kitchen where her mother was talking to the housekeeper.

She went down to the stilt house and let herself in. It felt odd being there when Summer was away—sneaky, dishonest, like she'd have a hard time explaining herself if anyone discovered her. But Summer was far away, and Diana was confident that Diver would not be around. Summer said he only appeared late at night and early in the morning.

She got what she needed and left, feeling the weight of the bag on her shoulder.

She took her own car and drove to the Merrick estate, all the while going over and over what she had to say, how she had to act, the things she had to be careful *not* to say.

The Merrick mansion loomed huge and intimidating as she parked her tiny Neon between a silver-and-black Rolls Royce and a mean, low-slung red Viper.

I should be afraid, Diana realized. I should be shaking, trembling, the way I was the last time I was here. But as she took internal inventory, she knew she wasn't afraid. Or if fear was present, it had been transformed somehow, had assumed a new and utterly different shape.

She took a deep, calming breath and got out. At the door she pressed the buzzer. Then she slipped her hand under the tail of her blouse. And, finally, she squeezed her bag.

"Do it, Diana," she muttered under her breath. "Do it."

The door opened. She'd expected Manolo, the butler. It was Ross. He leered cockily at her, and she took a step back, shocked.

Of course. They had deliberately sent Ross, thinking it would unsettle her. She reminded herself of what she had told herself a thousand times already—these were the Merricks. They were experts at using power and intimidation.

"Hello, Ross," she said.

"Why, it's Diana," he said. "What a surprise." He leaned close, to whispering distance. "Come back to get more of what I started to give you?"

"I'm here to see your father," Diana said, fighting down the feeling of loathing. The burning anger deep inside her flared. Good. Anger was her friend.

She followed Ross down the hall, past the gloomy portraits of Merricks past. He led her to a room she'd never been in before, a huge, dark, walnut-paneled library with stacks of leather-bound books. More clever intimidation, she noted, another attempt to make her feel ill at ease.

She felt like laughing. The Merricks didn't realize that they were not dealing with the same Diana they'd known. Not anymore.

Ross pointed to a single chair positioned before a massive desk. Diana sat stiffly, legs crossed. She rested her bag on her leg, holding it tight.

Adam entered the room, dressed in well-weathered but still spotless jeans, and a pale yellow shirt. She recognized the shirt. She had given it to him, part of an attempt to broaden his preppy clothing choices.

"Hi, Diana," he said quietly. "It's good to see you again."

For a split second Diana almost believed the warmth in his voice. Almost.

"I'm sure you're thrilled that I'm here," Diana said dryly.

Then the senator came in. He was a big, impressive man, wearing an expensively tailored suit that did not conceal his beefy shoulders or his spreading waistline. But the good looks he'd passed on to his sons was still in evidence.

He took a long look at her as he stood behind his desk, surveying her with open disdain.

It would have worked, Diana realized. Even two weeks ago, a week ago, she would have collapsed. His look, loaded with contempt, would have found resonance in her own mind. Even now she could feel that dark, twisted part of her endorsing his contempt, knowing, as he knew, that she was unworthy to be sitting here.

But Diana reached out for the new feeling she had allowed to grow. Anger. She let it flare and grow hot, and felt the power of it.

The senator sat down. His sons arranged themselves on either side of him. He waved a hand toward her. "You had something to say?"

"Yes, I did," Diana said.

"Well, let's hear it," the senator said. He glanced at his watch. "What's this about?"

"This is about rape."

"*Attempted* rape," Ross broke in. His father silenced him with a cold glare. The look surprised Diana. She'd thought the senator had treated *her* with contempt. But the frozen look he'd sent his son showed he was capable of much greater scorn.

Diana reminded herself to stay steady. She had a game plan worked out. So far it was still on track.

"Maybe it was just *attempted* rape," Diana said. "But maybe it would make a much more interesting story if I left out the word *attempted*."

"You lying bitch!" Ross exploded.

"Diana," Adam said much more calmly, cutting his brother off, "you know that's not true. I was there. I know that didn't happen. There is no point in trying to pretend that more happened than actually did."

"Sure, there's a point, all right," Ross sneered. "She's thinking she can squeeze us for more money if she makes it look worse than it was."

"Shut up, Ross." The senator's voice was like a knife. He breathed deeply and ran his tongue over his teeth while he favored Diana with a new look—amusement. "Yes, I suppose you *are* right," he said, chuckling softly. "It would make a better story that way. I guess for once I should actually be glad that Ross failed to follow through on what he started. He's had so many failures."

"What is it you want, Diana?" Adam asked.

"They always want the same thing," the senator said dryly. "You'll learn that eventually, Adam. When you are rich, all anyone ever wants from you is money. Did you have a dollar amount in mind, Diana?"

"Did *you*, Senator?" Diana shot back.

The man laughed out loud. "Oh, Adam, you really should have found a way to hold on to this one," he said. "What a perfect political wife she would have made. It's a useful thing to have a smart, ruthless, and, may I say, beautiful wife at your side." But Adam looked troubled. He was gazing narrowly at Diana, sensing that something was wrong. He had known her too long and too well. "She doesn't want money," he said.

"Then, what?" Ross demanded.

"You, Ross," Diana said through gritted teeth. "I want you. In prison."

Ross barked a wild laugh. "You *are* crazy. You think you're going to put a Merrick in prison?" Unable to control himself any longer, he jumped around the corner of the desk, lunging toward Diana. "You want to mess with me?" he shouted. "I'll finish what I started with you last year! I'll finish it right now."

Diana jumped up from her chair, just as Ross thrust out a hand to grab her. Suddenly everything was in motion.

Adam came around the desk from his side. But the senator, old as he was, was closer, and surprisingly fast. He reached Ross first. He swung his fist and buried it in Ross's stomach.

Ross fell to the floor, gasping for breath and clutching his stomach. He looked stunned and horrified. But no more horrified than Adam.

"Dad, Dad!" Adam took his father by his shoulders, restraining him and comforting him, too.

"Now do you see?" Diana screamed, shaking with rage and fresh terror. "Do you see what he is? Do you see what your son is, Senator?"

"Yes, damn it, I know what he is," the senator

bellowed, in a voice that seemed to make the room vibrate. "Do you think I've lived this long and still don't recognize garbage when I see it?" Diana could only stand there, unable to think of anything to say. This was not in the plan. Ross was gagging and gasping on the floor, still doubled over.

The senator yanked at his cuffs and straightened his jacket. Then, more quietly, "I know what Ross is. Yes. I know."

"Dad, come on," Adam said, now near tears. He guided his father back to his chair. "Come on, Dad, don't do this to yourself."

Ross crawled away, then carefully, still clutching his stomach, slowly rose far enough to slide into a chair.

For a while no one said anything. Diana sat back down in her seat. She clutched the bag again on her knee.

"Here it is, young lady," the senator said. His voice was flat now, empty of any emotion. "If you try to charge my son with any crime or accuse him publicly of any crime, I will use every bit of my power and influence to destroy you. I'll have every minute of your life investigated. I'll investigate your family, your friends. Maybe I'll find something incriminating, maybe not—it doesn't matter. Because one way or another, I'll destroy you. I *own* the prosecutor here, she was elected with my support, and she'll do what I say. The same with the local police. Chief Dorman is a personal friend of mine. You won't find anyone who will believe you or support you. And in the end you'll be made to look like a hysterical, pathetic figure."

As this speech went on, Diana noticed Adam's face growing sadder. He looked steadily down at the floor. She almost thought he might be crying. Ross just sat silently. At last, it seemed, it had penetrated his mind that he was in trouble, and being rescued by a father who was sickened by the necessity of saving him.

"On the other hand," the senator said, "we can forget all of this. And you can have a check for enough money to pay your way through any college in the country, and have a nicely furnished apartment off-campus, and a nice little sports car to drive back and forth to classes. Those are your choices—walk away with a fat check, or get a lesson in the influence of a senior senator with a great deal of money."

He pushed back from the desk and stood up. "Think about it for twenty-four hours. Let me know what you decide. Adam, see her to the door."

Adam walked with her down the long hallway. They walked in silence. Diana just felt numb. It had worked. She had not failed. She had not broken down. She had not succumbed to fear but had let her anger guide her.

But it was a strange feeling, winning. More melancholy than happy.

Adam walked with her out onto the front steps and stopped. It was hot and bright and there was a soft breeze blowing from the water.

"Diana," Adam said.

"Yes?"

He moved with sudden speed, grabbed one arm, and, with his free hand, fumbled for the tape player in her belt. He yanked it out. He looked at it and nodded, as if he'd expected it all along.

Diana froze.

"My dad said you'd try something like this," Adam said. "He told me to be sure to get it away from you."

He pushed the Rewind button, then Play. Ross's voice.

". . . to mess with me? I'll finish what I started with you last year!"

Adam clicked it off. Then he held it out to her.

Diana took the tape player from him. She searched his face for some explanation, but he would not meet her gaze.

"Adam, tell your father I have made up my mind," Diana said.

"I know," he said.

17

Black Holes

*D*own, down they went, deeper than they had ever gone before. Sunlight, so brilliant above on the surface, was filtered and pale at this depth, like a light from another world.

They played a slow-motion game of tag, Summer following Seth through forests of seaweed, around miniature mountain ranges of tumbled rock and fabulous extrusions of coral, pausing to watch an eel warily poking its nose out of its lair, sharing a moment of pretended terror at the appearance of a small, harmless baby lemon shark. Seth had brought his speargun and looked unusually fierce, prowling the ocean floor with it held casually in his left hand. He was determined, he said, to spear their dinner.

Summer watched a huge crab, or what looked like a crab to her, shoot backward, stirring up a little whirlpool of sand in its wake. She grabbed Seth's leg and pointed. Better than spearing some poor helpless fish, she decided. Somehow that would have felt wrong.

Seth nodded. Crabmeat would be fine by him. He went off in pursuit.

The crab went straight into a fissure in the rocks. The fissure was large, and Seth cautiously stuck his head in, probing the darkness with the tip of his speargun.

He motioned for Summer to shine the underwater flashlight inside. She floated alongside him and aimed the beam inside. The light played around crusted walls and caught the retreating crab.

Seth turned to face her and made a wide, encompassing gesture with his arms. She took it that he was telling her the cave was big. Then he shrugged, not dismissively, but more in a "how about it?" way.

Summer automatically checked her watch. She still had thirty minutes of air. More than enough. But the idea of swimming into the cave scared her. She made a back-and-forth gesture with her head— "not sure."

He held up a finger—"look." He unwrapped a length of yellow nylon rope and fastened one end around a large bulb of coral. Then, with hand gestures, Seth explained that they would go in only as far as the rope would go. That way, there would be no danger of becoming lost inside.

Summer nodded. Yes. She was up for it.

Seth winked and led the way through the fissure.

It was narrow enough that they could go through only one at a time. Summer kept the flashlight trained on Seth, spotlighting his dull-gray tank, a flash of flipper, a tan, muscular leg.

She realized she was breathing too fast, unnerved by the suddenly confined space. She bumped against the wall and heard a scraping sound.

Then it leapt at her, a lightning-quick strike that was just a blur in the water. She screamed into her regulator. The eel slapped hard against the side of her face, dislodging her mask. Water rushed in, blinding her.

She recoiled, paddling back in panic. Her tank slammed hard into the low roof of the cave.

She had the sense of an arm, feeling for her, missing. Then the eel whipped across her stomach.

The light fell away, turning down through the water, a strange slow-motion firework. It came to rest in the sand, pointing uselessly at the wall of the cave.

She tried to calm herself, but now something else had brushed against her leg. Blind and in terror she twisted hard, slamming her tank again against the low roof.

There was a muffled cracking sound, like splintering wood or distant thunder.

Something heavy dropped on the back of her legs. She kicked and moved out of its way. She had lost one of her fins. Something else struck her arm. Another sharp, hard object grazed her left thigh.

She swam forward with all her strength and plowed directly into something soft and yielding. Seth! His arms found her in the darkness and held her close, gripping her like a vise, forcing her to stop moving.

For a while she just waited, listening to the scraping, sliding sounds behind her, trying to slow the panicked beat of her heart, trying to gain control over the panting that seemed to bring less and less air from the regulator.

Seth tapped gently on her face mask. He was telling her to clear her mask, to blow out the water so that she would be able to see. She did, and realized it was not completely black in the cave. A few feet below was the flashlight. Seth dived to get it. But there was some other light, too, very faint but definite.

Seth aimed the flashlight back at the entrance to the cave. It was gone.

The yellow nylon rope went to, and then through, a jumbled wall of fallen rock.

They were trapped. Summer felt the panic beginning to rise in her chest again. Seth came over and patted her on the shoulder. He handed her the light, and she directed it as he worked to dislodge the fallen rocks.

He was able to toss aside a dozen small stones. But one huge slab of rock lay unmovable.

Seth tried by himself, and with Summer's desperate help, but the slab would not budge.

Finally, Seth pointed to her gauge. Ten minutes

of air left. He looked at his own watch and held up seven fingers. In about seven minutes he would be out of air. Three minutes later her own air would be gone.

The thought of those three minutes shook Summer Smith like nothing she had ever felt before.

Diana arrived back at her house feeling weird and disconnected from everything that had just happened. It was as if she were watching herself park the car, watching herself go inside, watching herself watching herself from a long way off.

What had it all meant? On one level it was easy to understand—she had succeeded in getting hard proof of what Ross had done a year earlier. For a year she'd felt beaten and defeated. She'd lived without hope, spiraling down and down, into "the hole," as she'd called it, the deep, black hole of depression.

And then, almost at the last minute, she'd seen the way out of the hole. She'd seen that the Merricks were afraid, and that had allowed her anger, for so long turned inward, to explode outward, directed at a better target.

She should feel wonderful. She felt nothing at all.

Her mother was in the living room and called to her as she passed by.

"You're back early," Mallory said. She sounded tense.

"It didn't take long," Diana said absently.

"What didn't take long?" her mother asked, speaking in clipped, angry cadences. "It didn't take long for you to try to blackmail Senator Merrick?"

Diana literally staggered. She looked at her mother with pure, undisguised horror. "How—"

"The senator called me, how do you think? I just hung up the phone with him." Mallory stood up and marched over to Diana. She grabbed her arm hard and dragged her to the couch. She practically flung her daughter into it.

"Do you want to tell me what in hell you think you're up to?" Mallory demanded.

"Didn't Merrick already tell you?"

"I want to hear it from *you*, Diana. Because I'm hoping that you have some good explanation for the fact that you are trying to blackmail a United States senator, for God's sake!"

Her mother was screaming at her. Literally screaming, in a voice Diana hadn't heard her use since the divorce. A wild, bitter, sarcastic voice.

"I'm not blackmailing anyone," Diana said weakly. She felt as if the air were being crushed out of her, as if she couldn't breathe. All she wanted to do was run away.

"Don't lie to me," Mallory exploded. "I'm not that stupid, Diana. I know when I'm being lied to. Senator Merrick himself called me and told me what you were up to. Are you trying to tell me that *he* is making this up?"

Diana wanted to speak, but her throat was one

big lump. Tears were filling her eyes, threatening to spill over. She was determined not to cry in front of her mother.

"Diana," Mallory said in a slightly less hostile tone, "I know you're young, but this is still inexcusable. Do you have any idea what that old man can do to me? To us?"

"He can't do anything to *me*," Diana said, forcing the words out through gritted teeth. She needed to find her own anger again. Needed to hold on to it.

"Oh, can't he?" her mother sneered. "You pathetic little creature, don't you know? Don't you know anything? Are you that ignorant? Who do you think pays for this house and your clothes and your cute little car? I do. *I* do."

Diana shook her head in puzzlement. What was her mother ranting about?

"Oh, I see—you don't get the connection?" Mallory said with savage sarcasm. "Well, here's the connection. My publisher is owned twenty-five percent by a company called M.H.G. You know what M.H.G. is? The Merrick Holdings Group. You know how much influence a twenty-five percent share buys? Plenty. More than enough to cut my throat professionally."

Diana felt sick. She feared she might throw up from the churning in her stomach. Her head was spinning. She'd thought she'd won. She'd thought she had outsmarted the Merricks. Now they were showing her that the battle had only begun. They had reached right into her home, threatening the one thing her mother really cared about—her career.

Mallory laughed derisively. "You thought you could blackmail someone like Senator Merrick? Do you need money that badly? I'd have given you money. Rather than have you making up ridiculous stories . . ."

Diana felt her lip quivering. Tears were spilling now, and she was past worrying about them. "It isn't a story," she said. She pulled the tape recorder out of her waistband. She pushed the button, and sat the recorder on the seat beside her.

The voices were hollow-sounding but clear. The entire conversation had recorded plainly, except for a few scratching noises.

Mallory turned away, listening, hiding her face.

Diana sat very still, saying nothing, vaguely interested in the words, feeling as if she were listening to a conversation that had taken place somewhere else, involving people she didn't know.

The tape came to an end.

Mallory walked the few steps to her daughter. With one hand she picked up the tape recorder. With the other she absently stroked her daughter's head.

Then she went to the coffee table and sat down. Methodically she pulled the tape from the cartridge, piling the loops in a crystal ashtray.

Diana watched her mother in horror, unable to move. *You can't do this!* she wanted to scream, but no words came out.

Mallory picked up a matching crystal cigarette lighter and touched the flame to the tape. "I'm doing this for your own good," she said.

Diana sat passively. Her anger was gone. She felt nothing. Nothing at all.

The black hole opened beneath her, welcoming her back.

18

Running Out of Time

Ten minutes of air. Ten minutes. Not a long time for Summer to think about all the things she would never know in her life. Her short life, down suddenly to ten minutes.

Seth patted her shoulder. She held his hand and squeezed it tight.

Once more Summer swept the beam around them. Walls of stone and crusted shellfish surrounded them, except in one direction where the cave went down deeper still. The huge crab they had chased was nowhere to be seen. The yellow nylon rope disappeared into the crush of fallen rocks, as if it had gone off into another dimension entirely.

Summer wondered if the flashlight battery would last as long as their air. Probably. Ten minutes—no, nine—was not a long time.

Then she remembered it. The light. The *other* light.

She turned off the flashlight. Seth shook her, telling her to turn it back on, but she squeezed his hand again to signal that she had a reason. Slowly her eyes adjusted to the darkness. Once again, she was able to make out dim shapes.

Now Seth had noticed it, too. There should be no light at all.

She snapped the flashlight on again, pointing it at Seth, then directing the beam along the cave floor. Seth nodded. His eyes were worried but determined. He set off at a moderate speed with Summer close behind. They followed the sandy cave floor down several more feet, reaching a point where the cave roof almost closed off further progress.

The end of the rope was played out now. Seth used a loose bit of rock to anchor it to the cave floor. Then he went through the narrow opening. Summer followed, careful not to scrape the rock.

They were in a larger cavern, how large it was impossible to say. But the cave roof was too far overhead even to be seen in the flashlight beam. Summer turned the flashlight off again.

Hope! The emotion surged in her heart. There was light overhead. Filtered, dim as earliest gray dawn, but definite light. She started up. Seth restrained her, shaking his head slowly.

Summer understood. They could not shoot suddenly upward. The decompression would cause the bends, a very painful form of death. Even now, they had to be careful.

They rose slowly, slowly, fighting the panicky urge to hurry.

Suddenly, Summer realized, her head was out of the water. It seemed unbelievable. But when she raised her mask cautiously, it was true. Air. Genuine, breathable air.

"Thank God," she gasped. "There's air."

There was air but no sunlight. Where *were* they?

Seth surfaced beside her and tore off his own mask. He swiftly shut the valves on their tanks. "We're in some kind of air pocket," he said.

Summer trained the flashlight around. They were in a huge, vaulted cavern, with sheer rock walls on three sides. On the other side the rock rose more gradually, creating a low, jumbled, dry shelf before it continued up and up.

At the very apex of the cavern was a tiny window of brilliant blue. The sky.

Seeing it brought tears to Summer's eyes. The sky.

Seth was laughing, a relieved, tired, half-hysterical laugh. Summer realized she was laughing, too, even as tears blurred her vision.

Seth looked at his gauge. "Three minutes," he said. "I was on fumes."

Summer swam to the shelf and pulled herself heavily out of the water. "Air," she said. "Boy, do I love air."

Seth slumped exhausted beside her. "Air is

excellent," he agreed. He sat up and looked around. "Of course, stairs or a ladder would be nice, too. We're beneath the island now. I guess this is basically an underground lake."

"There has to be some way to get up there," Summer said. But as she surveyed the cave her confidence faded quickly. The patch of sky was high, very high overhead. The cave was like an overturned bowl, sides sloping upward, utterly impossible to climb unless you were a spider.

"Someone will come," Seth said, trying to sound confident. "You know, other divers. They'll see the boat, and then if they go down, they'll see the rope. They'll figure out about the cave-in."

Summer nodded in agreement. "You're probably right."

They both stared up at the patch of blue.

"We won't freeze or anything," Seth said. "I mean, it's a little chilly here, but with the wet suit tops . . ."

"And we have air," Summer said. "A few minutes ago I thought I would gladly sell my soul for fresh air. Or stale air. Or for a chance to suck on bus exhaust. I've never been so terrified."

"Yeah," he agreed. "Look, I'm sorry about getting you into this."

"You? Jeez, I'm the one who panicked and caused an avalanche or whatever it was."

"A cave-in," he said glumly. "Cave. Cave-in."

"That makes sense," she said, echoing his grim tone.

"It's *my* fault, not yours," he said.

"Let's not argue about it," Summer said. The adrenaline was wearing off now, and lassitude was setting in. She wanted to savor the sense of relief a little longer before having to move on to recognizing that they were still in serious trouble.

"Why not argue about it?" Seth said. "We have plenty of time."

They fell silent and stared up at the patch of blue. Already it seemed the light was fading, the blue growing darker, shading toward violet.

The dinner shift had been busy. Marquez had more than a hundred dollars in tips weighing down the pocket of her apron. And she still had a deuce sitting out in the dining room as she began her side work, cleaning the salad and soup area in the kitchen. The job involved emptying the sloppy, destroyed containers of salad dressing they'd used all night into new containers and topping them off from the big bins in the walk-in.

In the old days she'd liked this job. It gave her an opportunity to be in the kitchen and make frequent trips to the walk-in, where J.T. would manage to be at the same time. It was a little game they played, meeting, kissing, then going back out to work to start the cycle over again. It had been strangely exciting.

Now she minimized her opportunities to run into J.T. He did the same, steering clear of her.

He had come over at one point to apologize for

the scene in the dining room the night before. She'd apologized, too. Yes, they had both agreed, they were acting immature.

She'd told him that she was glad if Lianne was good for him. He'd asked her if she had found anyone, and she'd lied and said that she was seeing someone. She stopped short of telling him it was Diver. That lie was too easy to check out, and then she would just look pathetic.

Despite the hundred and two dollars she had after paying out the bartender and the busboys, she felt low when she left the Crab 'n' Conch. Low and restless. She went home and called Summer. No answer. Too bad. Summer would have picked up her spirits.

She showered and called Summer again. Still no answer. If the girl was in the bathroom or something, she was certainly taking her time. Marquez glanced at the clock. Almost a quarter after eleven. Summer had to be back from her trip by now.

Maybe she had disconnected her phone. Maybe she didn't want to be disturbed. Maybe she and Seth were . . .

"That's right, Marquez," she muttered, "torture yourself. Everyone is having a great time but you."

But no, Summer wouldn't have Seth still over at the house. Diver would be there by now, and Summer wasn't the kind of girl who would feel comfortable making out while someone was snoozing on her roof. Marquez considered calling Diana, but her mom was back and might pick up the phone. The last thing Summer needed was Mallory Olan bursting into the stilt house looking for her.

Marquez decided to go by and check for herself. There was probably nothing to worry about. And maybe she would run into Diver. They had gotten off to a bad start the other day. Marquez had been too aggressive. She'd forgotten that Diver was different from most guys.

"Different from most humans, for that matter," Marquez said. Of course, right now J.T. was probably baring his soul and whatever else he could get away with baring to Lianne. Maybe Marquez should give Diver another chance.

She looked at the white patch on her wall. The white paint covering the letters J.T. "Jerk," she said to the patch. And yet, she wished she hadn't painted his name out. It was easier to be mad at a name than a blank patch.

She drove her parents' car to the Olan house, parking down the street rather than in the driveway. She walked quietly past the main house, feeling relieved when she reached the stilt house unchallenged.

The stilt house was dark and silent, the only sounds the slap of water against the pilings and the slow, mournful creak of the pier.

She considered turning back. Obviously Summer was just asleep, exhausted from the long day. "Well, tough," Marquez muttered. "She'll just have to wake her little self up."

Marquez knocked on the door.

She was startled by a voice from above.

"She's not here." Diver, a dark shape, standing on the deck, looking down.

Even now Marquez remembered his brief kiss, just a brush of his perfect lips against hers. Maybe they just needed to try that a second time. Or . . . maybe not.

"She went out?"

"I don't think so," Diver said. His voice sounded troubled.

"You mean she never came home?" Marquez opened the door, reached in and flipped on a light. The bed was made, a surprising sight to Marquez, who never actually made her own bed.

"Summer? You home?" She looked into the bathroom, the only separate room.

Diver dropped down behind her and followed Marquez inside.

"I don't think she's been back," Marquez said. She felt out of place, as if the familiar surroundings had become different somehow.

"She hasn't been back," Diver said. "I'm sure."

"Diver, you're worrying me," Marquez said.

"I'm worried," he said. "I—I feel she may be in trouble."

"It's almost midnight. She should have gotten back hours ago. She went scuba diving with Seth. You don't think anything could have happened, do you?"

"Yes," he said. "I do think something happened."

"Oh my God. What should we do?" Marquez wondered. "Should I tell Mrs. Olan? Or call the Coast Guard?"

"What can Mrs. Olan do?" Diver asked. "Maybe the Coast Guard."

"Yeah, you're right. She'd just get all upset and it's probably nothing. But we could call the Coast Guard and, you know, find out if . . . if they've picked up any boats out of gas or whatever."

Diver nodded solemnly. He seemed to have withdrawn even further inside himself than usual.

Suddenly the atmosphere in the room seemed frightening to Marquez. As if the temperature had dropped. "I'll call the Coast Guard," she said briskly, anxious to be doing something.

"I guess that's all we *can* do," Diver said.

But another possibility had occurred to Marquez. A possibility that had to do with burned hands and two people talking at the very same moment. "There's another person who might be able to help, too," Marquez said.

Diana lay in her bed, uncovered, wearing a simple, white gauze shift, watching the numbers on the clock change. Eleven thirty-eight to eleven thirty-nine. She was waiting for midnight. Midnight seemed right. She didn't know why. It was just that she had to pick some time, some definite time, when she would do it. Midnight was definite.

She tightened her grip on the small brown bottle. Her palm was dry, not sweating with nerves.

She didn't feel nervous. Hadn't felt nervous when she took the bottle from her mother's bathroom. Her mother had not noticed it missing from her medicine cabinet.

Or perhaps she had noticed it and just didn't care.

Mallory had burned the tape, saying it was for Diana's own good. Maybe she even halfway believed it. But Diana knew that her own good was no longer an issue. There would be no good for Diana. She was no longer part of the world that others inhabited. The world that Summer—and Seth—lived in.

She had been lying here forever, it seemed, indifferent to the failing light, indifferent to falling night. Thinking of nothing. Feeling nothing but the presence of the hole as she fell and fell and fell into it, deeper and deeper, like Alice in Wonderland. Too far even to hope for a way back out.

She had fallen all the way down the hole. And she had found no last-minute salvation. At the end of it all, she was alone. Alone with herself.

"Just me," Diana whispered. "Just me."

Eleven-forty. Twenty minutes to go.

19

Late News and News Too Late

J.T.'s apartment was a tiny, unexceptional place, with two windows over the main drag, upstairs from a kite store. He had a small balcony off to one side, and the people who owned the store had him hang brightly colored kites from it. He had moved in at the beginning of the summer, wanting to have more independence and freedom than he had in his parents' home. The thought had also been that he and Marquez could enjoy some privacy there.

A set of exterior wooden steps led up to the apartment. Marquez climbed them quietly, not wanting to wake J.T. prematurely. She was still undecided about whether to wake him up at all. It was a fairly amazing thing she would have to lay on him, if she decided to go ahead. Her natural reluctance to get further into other people's problems inclined her to walk away. But it was after midnight, and Summer still wasn't home.

She knocked on the door and only then considered the possibility that Lianne might be inside with J.T.

"That would certainly be embarrassing," she said under her breath. But then, one way or the other, this was not going to be an easy visit to J.T.

She had to knock three different times, louder each time, before she saw a light go on inside. The ratty little curtain in the door window moved slightly. J.T. appeared, squinting out of one eye, the other scrunched closed. When he saw her, he opened the other eye as well. Then he opened the door.

"I suppose you're wondering why I'm here in the middle of the night?" Marquez said brightly. J.T. was wearing pajama bottoms and no shirt.

"It crossed my mind, yeah," he said. He scratched his hair, which just made a bigger mess of it. He seemed to be tasting something he didn't like.

"It's about Summer," she said.

He thought about this for a moment. "The waitress or the season?"

"Summer Smith. She's not at home."

He nodded. "Summer's not at home. Okay. Thanks for coming by and telling me. I'd been tossing and turning in bed, asking myself: do you think Summer is at home or not? You've cleared that up for me."

"Can I come in?" Marquez asked, letting his sarcasm flow past without a response.

He shrugged and led the way inside. The apartment was a typical "guy" apartment—a few sticks of furniture, a large quantity of dirty clothing, posters sagging on the walls, a stone-dead potted plant.

J.T. went to the kitchen, reappearing with a carton of orange juice from which he took several long swallows.

Marquez took the one chair. J.T. sat on the edge of the bed and scratched himself indiscreetly.

"Sorry," he mumbled, when he saw her disapproving look. "So, Summer isn't home. What's the rest of the secret message?"

"She went out early this morning with Seth Warner. They were going to some island to do some diving. They were supposed to be home this evening. They aren't home yet."

This penetrated. J.T. was a diver himself. He nodded seriously. "Could be engine problems with the boat," he said. "That's most likely. Or maybe they lost track of time and decided to sleep over on the island. It isn't necessarily something . . . bad."

"I called the Coast Guard. They said the same things, but they also said they'd put out an alert." Marquez hesitated. So far she hadn't told J.T. anything troubling. She hadn't passed the point of no return.

"Why did you come here?" J.T. asked. "Getting

my expert opinion as a diver? I'm not exactly a professional. You've already called the C.G. It's probably like they said."

Oh, well, Marquez realized, there was probably no avoiding it. "But what do *you* think it is?" Marquez asked, leaning forward in her chair.

"I have no idea," J.T. said.

Marquez took a deep breath. Then another. This was going to be strange. "Um, J.T., I don't know how much you've ever talked to Summer . . ."

"Not much. You know, just work gossip."

"So I guess she never told you about . . . about Jonathan." Okay, *now* she was past the point of no return.

J.T. looked impatient. "You know, Marquez, I was thinking sleep might not be a bad thing."

"He was her brother. Jonathan. He disappeared when he was two years old. Before Summer was even born. They never found out what happened to him."

Suddenly J.T. was sitting very still. His eyes were narrowly focused on Marquez's face.

Marquez plunged ahead. "The other day at work, I noticed that you burned yourself, and at the exact same moment, Summer burned herself in the same place. I know this seems crazy, just let me finish. There was another time when Summer was complaining she had a headache and you had a headache, too. And then the other day, when you both said exactly the same thing at exactly the same time—"

"How old is Summer?" he asked in a quiet voice.

"She's seventeen, I guess. She said her brother disappeared just a couple of months before she was born."

"Which would mean, if he's alive today, he would be about eighteen, maybe just turned nineteen," J.T. said.

"Yeah," Marquez confirmed.

"My age."

"Your age."

"How long have you suspected this?" he asked.

"I don't know, a week, I guess," Marquez said. "It seemed totally insane. But tonight I got to thinking, you know, about the burning and the headache and all. You know, people talk about brothers and sisters having these . . . these connections, you know?"

J.T.'s calm facade began to break down. He looked overwhelmed, like he wanted to hide somewhere. He rubbed his face with his palms.

"I thought, I don't know, you might have some idea, some feeling about whether she's in trouble." Marquez threw up her hands. "Sorry. This is insane. I can't believe I even said anything. This is nuts."

"Do you know what this would mean?" J.T. asked, his face stricken. "Do you know what it would mean for my parents? I mean, are they some kind of kidnappers? Is that what I'm supposed to believe?"

"I don't know," Marquez said. She fidgeted in her seat for a minute, trying to decide what to do.

J.T. kept rubbing his face. It was becoming a compulsive movement now, one he couldn't seem to stop.

Marquez got up and went to sit beside him. She carefully did not touch him and kept her hands folded in her lap. "Look, J.T., I know this is a lot to even think about. I wouldn't have said anything, except I'm worried about Summer. The girl seems to have a talent for getting herself into one kind of mess or another."

"I don't have any idea where she is," J.T. said distractedly. "How would I know? This is nuts. You're right, this *is* insane. I mean, I'm not having some kind of psychic connection, if that's what you think."

"But could you maybe *think* about it?" Marquez pleaded.

J.T. made an effort to focus. "Look, as a diver I can tell you that there are only a couple of good diving places where they could have gone in an open boat from here and gotten back in the same day."

"That's something, at least," Marquez said.

He laughed bitterly. "Marquez, if they're in serious trouble, that information is worth nothing. They probably went down with about an hour of air. An hour."

"I know," Marquez said, "but I have to try, right?" She jumped up to try to find a shirt and pants for him to put on.

J.T. managed a small, wistful smile. "You getting in the middle of other people's problems, Marquez?"

Marquez concentrated on digging through a pile of dirty clothes. "I guess staying *out* of other people's problems doesn't always work out that great, either."

The patch of blue was no more than a distant memory. Now only two faint stars were visible through the hole above. Summer was hungry and thirsty, despite the fact that Seth had showed her how to lick condensation from the rocks.

Worse than hungry or thirsty, she was afraid.

It was dark in the cave. Totally dark, since they were conserving their precious flashlight. So dark that Summer could literally not see her hand in front of her face.

There was no way out. They had spent hours trying to think of a way to escape. But there was no escape. None. And it was too easy to conjure up images of two rubber-clad skeletons being found down here someday.

"I wonder which stars those are," Seth said.

He was just a voice, nearby in the total darkness. Not a happy voice.

"Someone told me once that stars weren't really far away," Summer said. "That they were right here."

"I guess that's true of the starlight," Seth said. "It's right here."

Summer smiled sadly in the darkness. Poor Diver. He'd wonder what happened to her. Or would he? He'd have the stilt house all to himself again.

"This summer vacation is not turning out quite the way I had planned," Summer said. There was a plopping sound in the water. Summer was used to it now. A fish, coming by to take a look at the odd phenomenon of two humans trapped like goldfish in a tank. "I kind of had this image of it just being sun and surf and parties."

"Sorry," Seth said softly.

"Sorry? Why are *you* sorry?" she said crossly.

"I got you into this," Seth said. "I helped get you into the mess with Ross and Adam. I've single-handedly ruined your life."

Summer thought for a while. "No, you didn't ruin anything. You've been the best part of this whole thing so far. Marquez and Diver, too, but mostly you."

"Don't be sweet to me," Seth said grimly. "I swear if you're nice to me I'll start crying."

"Crying wouldn't be so bad," Summer said. "I won't tell anyone. Ever," she added with deliberate dark humor.

"So much for my big theory that you and I were . . ." He sighed, an audible sound in the profound silence.

"That we were what?" Summer asked.

"You know," he said. "I told you already."

"Tell me again," she whispered.

"I had this feeling," he began. "It was so strong I

was sure it had to be real. It was like I could see the future, and I knew, totally, beyond any doubt, that you and I were going to be together."

"We *are* together," Summer said, trying to interject a weak note of levity.

"I had us going to college together and traveling around the world together, and I don't know, it sounds pretty idiotic now."

"No, it doesn't," Summer said.

"I even had us married someday, with kids and all that. A dog. I was thinking a Labrador. Maybe a mutt. It seemed so real. That first time, when we kissed, it was like 'Wake up, Seth, this is *her*. This is your one great love.'"

Summer stretched out her hand, searching for him. She touched his leg and from there found his hand. They linked their fingers together.

"You kind of scared me when you talked that way before," Summer confessed.

"It doesn't scare you now?"

"I have better things to be scared of," Summer pointed out. "But at the time I thought, you know, that if I got too involved . . . Jeez, I don't even know *what* I was thinking. That all seems like it was a completely different world. I was worried, you know, about committing. I thought if I didn't watch out I would fall totally in love with you, and then naturally it would end up in some kind of mess. That's how it always works."

"How it always works? What do you mean, like no one ever gets to be happy?"

"Not on the *Young and the Restless,*" Summer said. "Anytime a couple is happy it just means something terrible is coming. I mean, my parents were happy. They had my brother. And me on the way. And then suddenly it was time for something terrible to happen, and so it did."

"But, Summer, that doesn't mean it's a law of nature or something," Seth argued.

"Maybe not for everyone," Summer allowed.

"Not for you, either."

Summer hesitated before telling him any more. Wouldn't it just hurt him? Then again, they were probably going to die down here. If this wasn't a time for honesty, when was?

"See, it *did* happen," Summer said. "I was kind of falling for Adam. And look what happened."

There was a long silence. She wondered what his face would show, if she could see it.

"Yeah, but nothing happened to *you,*" Seth said. "I mean, it might have, but it didn't. Whereas *this* is a real mess." Again he was quiet for a while. "So if your idea is that being happy and in love is what leads to terrible things happening—"

"Then that would mean that I *was* in love and happy before this happened," Summer completed the thought. "See? Proof."

"Are you saying that— What are you saying?" he asked.

Summer sighed profoundly. "I tried not to let it happen," she said. "But it did. I fell in love with you, anyway. And then, boom, total disaster."

"You love me?" he asked, his voice soft and hopeful.

"Yes," Summer said. Then she raised his unseen hand to her lips, kissed it, and pressed it against her heart.

Seth shifted closer and put his arm around her shoulders. "Excellent timing, Summer," he said. "You couldn't fall in love with me *after* we went cave diving?"

"Sorry," she said, turning to him.

"Are you really sorry?" he asked, his lips close to hers.

And for a long time, no more words were spoken.

20

I Believe the Point Here
Is . . . Never Give Up.

*I*n her dream, Summer sat beside the tarot lady again. The tarot lady seemed not to want to meet her gaze, so in her dream, Summer was annoyed.

"So," she said accusingly, "you tell me all this stuff about these guys I'll meet, and you can't mention that maybe I should avoid small, damp, confined spaces?"

The tarot lady shuffled her cards. "Who knew?"

"Not you. Duh."

"The future is always shifting."

"Oh, that's perfect," Summer said. "Nice way to weasel out of it. You know what? No one can tell the future. All this stuff is just baloney. A big baloney sandwich. With cheese and mayonnaise and mustard and lettuce. And maybe it's a sub, one of those big Subway subs, what are they called . . . B.M.T.'s, yeah, all this different meat and have it with everything, even hot peppers—"

"You're hungry, aren't you?" the woman asked.

"I guess you can tell that from the cards," Summer said. "Let's see them. Turn them over. Stop keeping secrets from me."

The woman turned over a single card. It was the figure of a small boy, dressed all in white. He was holding something in his hand. A red ball.

"That card scares me," Summer said.

"Why?"

"You *know* why," she said. "Death. That's why, because he's dead. You're showing him to me because you think I'm going to die."

Suddenly Summer awoke. Her hair was standing on end.

She was in the cave still, she could tell from the sound of the water. She was in Seth's arms. The taste of his lips was still in her mouth. There was no light but for two stars far overhead, peeking through the hole in the roof.

Then she saw him—the boy in white. He was standing a little way off.

"Who are you?" Summer asked him in a whisper.

"I don't know," the little boy said. "I've been looking for you. For a long time."

Then the little boy threw a red ball, high, straight up. The ball flew up through the hole in the roof of the cave.

★   ★   ★

To her great surprise, Diana awoke.

She had not closed the curtains the night before because she had not expected to be worrying about being awakened by sunlight. But now the early-morning light was beaming directly into her eyes.

Diana blinked and squinted and looked around, confused. Why was she still here? Impossible. She'd decided to kill herself. She'd made up her mind to do it, at long last.

Diana realized she was holding something, clutched in her right hand. The brown pill bottle, the cap still securely in place. She opened her cramped, aching fingers, and the bottle rolled off onto the sheet.

She'd failed. She'd meant to kill herself, and instead she'd fallen asleep before she could take the pills. Fallen asleep before she could take the sleeping pills.

It was almost funny, she thought bitterly.

In fact, it *was* funny. She tried not to grin but couldn't help herself. She'd fallen asleep before she could take the fatal dose of sleeping pills.

"See, the thing is, I was *going* to kill myself," she said aloud, "but I was just too sleepy." Diana laughed. "If only I'd had another cup of coffee, I could be dead now."

Now what? Should she go back to sleep? Get up and take a shower? Kill herself?

She laughed some more. Shower or suicide? Hmm, there was a choice. And it brought up the question of whether, even if she *was* going to kill herself, she shouldn't take a shower first. "Who wants to die with morning breath and that grubby, unwashed feeling?"

She jumped out of bed and went to her porch door. She opened it and went outside. A slight morning breeze ruffled her sheer nightgown. It was almost cool out, not too humid, and the sun was still so low that it had not become the terror it would be by noon.

The water looked good. Maybe she should go for a swim.

"Then I can kill myself," she said, and immediately began laughing again.

"What is the matter with me?" she wondered aloud. Yesterday she'd been beaten down, falling back into the hole of depression. It was just too clichéd to think that because it was a nice day out she didn't want to kill herself. It was a nice day *every* day.

But it was too simplistic to think that she had just fallen asleep before she could carry out her plans. No. Something had to have changed her mind. Something had to have let her slip safely away into normal slumber.

The truth was, right now, with the warm deck under her feet and the sun on her face, she just didn't feel like killing herself.

"There. I admit it," she said to no one but herself.

She tried to think back to the night before, to lying in her bed, the bottle of pills in her hand, dark, dramatic images playing in her mind. The depression had been all around her then, had swallowed her whole. She remembered thinking that she couldn't ever trust her mother again. That she couldn't count on anyone or anything. That she had no one to turn to. That she was alone. Totally alone.

"That's right," she murmured, smiling sadly at the realization. She *was* totally alone. Maybe everyone was alone. Maybe that was the point. Maybe that's what she'd had to learn, that in the darkest times there wasn't anyone to turn to but yourself.

"What a sad thought," Diana whispered.

Let's face it, Diana, what are you? she asked herself. A sad, weak, screwed-up, inadequate person. No great genius. No great beauty. No perfect specimen of kindness or decency or morality. Sometimes a fool. Sometimes a jerk. Sometimes humiliated and pathetic.

All of it was true.

And yet, down at the bottom of that deep hole of depression, at the very end, whom had she found but herself? All alone. All alone with a messed-up person named Diana.

You're the only person I have, Diana told herself. The only person I am.

I guess you'll have to do.

She went back inside and retrieved the bottle of pills and carried it to the bathroom. She emptied the contents into the toilet bowl. "Bye," she said, and flushed.

She caught sight of herself in the mirror. The same reflection she'd looked at with loathing so many times. The memory brought tears to her eyes. She pointed a finger at herself. "You and me, kid."

For a long time she stood there, watching herself watching herself. Not bad-looking. Good hair. Not a complete idiot. Weak? Yes, she had been, for a long, long time. The reasons why she'd felt that way were tedious and obvious and probably unimportant—her absent, half-forgotten father, her unfortunately not absent mother . . . Ross. And Adam, the one guy she'd ever loved. Even more recently, the reproach represented by Summer and Seth—people she would never be, or have.

A long list of reasons to feel bad.

Her mouth twitched into a smile. Time to shorten up that long list.

In her bedroom she found the hideous shoulder bag. She poked her finger through the hole she'd cut into the fabric, the hole that was concealed by the awful pattern of the fabric.

She opened the bag. Yes, it was still there. Summer's video camera. The lens was duct-taped up against the hole.

She popped out the videocassette. Now to figure out how to make a copy. She wanted to keep the original.

Summer woke hungry. She woke hungry with her head resting on Seth's bare chest. She could tell from his breathing that he was already awake.

"Good morning," he said.

She slid up his body to give him a kiss. "Good morning," she said, several seconds later.

"I don't know how good a morning it's going to be," he said regretfully. "The night was good, though."

"Mmm," Summer said. "I'm starving."

"Well, there is the sushi option," Seth said. "We have the speargun, and we know we have fish trapped in here with us."

Summer shuddered. "I guess they eat sushi in Japan, right? And they seem to be doing okay."

"They eat it in Los Angeles and New York, too," Seth said. "Not so much in Eau Claire, Wisconsin."

"Or Bloomington, Minnesota," Summer said.

"What? Not even in the home of the Mall of America?" Seth joked.

"I wish I were there," Summer said. "They have all these fast-food places overlooking the amusement park. Hamburgers. Stuffed potatoes. Pizza. Mrs. Fields cookies. Fried chicken."

"Don't even say fried chicken," Seth groaned.

Summer forced herself to look around their hard, stony prison. It hadn't changed. It hadn't become any more comfortable. It was still a trap, and there was still no way out.

At the top of the dome, the same irregular patch of blue, lighter and brighter now than it had been yesterday. Outside in the world it was morning. Only this one small slice of morning made it inside of this cave, but it was still morning, and it was hard not to feel a little surge of hope.

"Okay," Summer said, "sushi it is."

Seth held her in his arms. "Do you still love me?" he asked.

"Still," Summer said.

"It isn't just because we're trapped and there's almost no hope of escape?"

Summer sighed. "That's how it's been since that first kiss in the airport, Seth. I've been trapped, and there was almost no hope of escape."

Seth grinned. So did Summer.

"Was that the corniest thing anyone's ever said to you?" Summer asked him.

"I believe it was," he said. "Now I'll tell you something even cornier—all this is worth it, because it brought us together, and that's worth anything."

"Even eating raw fish?"

He made a back-and-forth gesture with his hand.

It took an hour for Seth, wearing wet suit and just a snorkel, to spear a fish. He filleted it with his knife, laying out small bites of glistening white flesh on a clean rock.

The two of them stared at it.

"The Japanese love this stuff," Seth said.

"That's what I hear," Summer said.

The warm afterglow of early morning had worn off. Now Summer was facing a breakfast of raw fish, washed down with trickling condensation licked from the smooth rock walls of the cave.

"Seth, are we ever going to get out of here?"

"Sure," he said with hearty and phony enthusiasm. "Someone will see the boat, then they'll see the rope and dive down and realize that . . ." His optimism collapsed. "They'll figure even if we were diving here that we're dead by now. That's what they'll figure."

"Or the boat could have slipped its anchor and could be drifting on the current a hundred miles from here," Summer said.

For a while neither of them spoke. At last Seth picked up a piece of the fish. "I hear it's best when it's fresh," he said. He screwed up his face and popped it into his mouth. Slowly his expression changed. "Hey, this isn't bad."

"Yeah, right," Summer said.

"Seriously. It's no cheeseburger, but it's not gross, either."

Summer picked up a piece. "I guess I don't have much choice." She swallowed the piece whole without chewing. It wasn't awful. As long as she didn't think about it.

"Well, I guess we can survive awhile down here," Summer said grimly. "Licking the walls and eating raw fish. That's exactly what I had in mind for my summer vacation."

"Arrrrrggghhhh!" Seth suddenly exploded.

"What's the matter?" Summer cried.

Seth was pointing up at the patch of blue overhead. "What am I? An idiot? A moron?"

"Seth, what is it?"

"The speargun," he said. "The speargun. Jeez, am I slow sometimes. There's about twenty feet of rope on our side of the cave-in. We cut it, tie it around the spear shaft, and fire the spear up through the hole. If we're lucky it will wedge in the hole and we can climb up."

Summer stared at him. "That hole is too small for us to fit through."

"I know." He bit his lip. "But it's something. It's better than doing nothing."

Ten feverish minutes later, they were ready. Seth had used the last few minutes of air in his tank to retrieve the available rope. The yellow nylon cord was now tied firmly to the spear.

"Here goes nothing," Seth said. He took careful aim and fired the spear. On the first two attempts it missed and clattered futilely off the rock.

On the third try it sailed up, straight through the patch of sky.

Like the red ball, Summer realized. Like the little boy's red ball.

Marquez leaned over the side of the boat and plunged her face into the water. She kept her entire head under for a few seconds, letting the warm salt water soak her hair. Then she pulled back. The water had done nothing to wake her up. Maybe if it had been cold water . . .

She was bleary and exhausted. J.T. was no better. The two of them were depressed and miserable and stunned into stupidity. For most of the long, long night they had bickered and snapped at each other. But now they were both too tired for that.

"I don't see anything here," J.T. said. He was on the bow of the boat they'd borrowed from J.T.'s father, surveying the island through binoculars. "No boat. Nothing on the beach. There's what may be some footprints in the sand, but that isn't going to help us."

"Just like the others," Marquez said grimly. They had spent the night racing from one far-flung islet to the next. The more J.T. thought about it, the more plausible places he'd come up with where Seth and Summer might have gone. They had covered miles of black water under a starry sky. Miles without sleep and with less hope.

"Let's call the Coast Guard again," Marquez said. "Maybe they've found something."

"Go ahead," J.T. said.

Marquez keyed the radio handset and called the now-familiar signal for the Coast Guard station on Key West. "Hi, it's me again," she said without preliminary. They knew her by now.

The answer came, scratchy and metallic. "Ma'am, I do now have some data. We just got a message from the cutter. They've found a boat answering the description you gave."

Marquez's heart leapt. J.T. came running back to her. "They did?" Marquez asked shakily.

"Yes, ma'am. It was capsized, out in the channel, about nine miles southeast of Geiger Key. It looks like it may have been struck by a passing ship."

"Oh, my God," Marquez said.

"We're conducting an air and sea search in that area, looking for survivors."

"Oh, no," Marquez whispered. She handed the handset to J.T., who thanked the Coast Guardsman and signed off. Marquez collapsed on the vinyl-padded bench.

"It doesn't mean they're dead," J.T. said. "They could still be alive."

"Can you—" she pleaded. "Can you feel anything? I mean, do you have a sense that, one way or the other . . . ?"

J.T. looked sad. "Marquez, I told you. I don't really think I have some kind of psychic connection with Summer. Maybe she *is* my sister. But I can't do what you think I can." He sat beside her, miserable. "I wish I could."

Marquez patted his leg. "I don't even believe in stuff like that. Superstition and all."

He put his arm around her.

"This is bad," Marquez said.

"Yeah. This is bad," he agreed.

"You know, I don't like getting into other people's messes," she said.

"I may have known that about you," J.T. said ironically.

Marquez managed a slight smile. "Yes, I guess you did know that about me. And now, look, it's me who's dragged you into this mess. I could have kept my mouth shut. You'd have been sad, I mean, you knew Summer from work. But now it's like, you kind of find this sister, and then—"

"Don't give up yet," J.T. said.

"No, I won't give— Wait a second. Did you see that?"

"What?"

Marquez frowned and shook her head. No, she was just sleepy. Sleepy and seeing things that weren't there.

21

All Together Now: Hmm . . .

Summer climbed the rope. She was lighter than Seth, and smaller. She was more likely to fit through the tiny hole.

She used the gloves from her wet suit to help her grip with her hands. The hard part was gripping the slippery rope with her bare legs. The climb was difficult—nearly twenty feet straight up, though Seth was able to help lift her the first few feet.

Her arms were burning by the time she reached the top. The patch of blue grew larger, closer. Soon she would reach it, and then—

The spear bent in two. The rope collapsed. Summer fell, screaming in surprise and anger.

Seth caught most of her weight, and both of them fell to the floor of the cave. The bent spear clattered down and fell beside them. The coil of rope looped over them.

"Oh, God, can't anything work out?" Summer cried. She buried her face in her hands and began sobbing.

Seth seemed crushed. He said nothing, just hung his head.

A long time passed with no sound but Summer's soft sobbing and the plop of curious fish in the water.

"There's still hope," Seth began to say, but then he seemed unable to carry the thought any further.

"Hey. Anyone down there?"

For a moment Summer did not believe she'd heard it.

She looked up. The patch of blue was dark.

"Hey! Yes! We're down here!" Summer yelled.

"Is that you, Summer?"

"Marquez?" Summer said incredulously. "Marquez? Is that you?"

"Like I'm going to leave you here and end up having to work all your shifts? What the hell are you guys doing down there?"

"Eating sushi," Summer yelled back, convulsing with relieved laughter. Seth swept her up in his arms and spun her around again and again.

"*Eating sushi?* Is that supposed to mean something?" Marquez asked J.T.

It took only twenty minutes for the Coast Guard helicopter to arrive. The Guardsmen used picks and shovels to widen the hole in the top of the cave. Then they lowered a harness on the end of a winch.

The light in the real world was blinding after the

cave. Summer could not open her eyes at all for several minutes while Marquez hugged her and J.T. hugged her and various unknown Coast Guard guys hugged her.

Finally she scrunched open one eye and saw Marquez, looking ratty but beautiful. J.T. was standing there, looking unusually shy.

"How are you guys?" Marquez asked.

"Great," Seth said. "Excellent fun. We'll really have to do this again someday, like when hell freezes over. By the way, did you guys see the boat?"

"No. The boat got loose. I hope it's insured," J.T. explained. "I guess it got in the way of a tanker."

"So how did you find us? I mean, how did you even know we were here?" Seth asked.

"Marquez saw something come flying up out of the ground, right here," J.T. said. "She said it looked like an arrow with a yellow snake attached. We were just getting ready to give up."

"As for how we picked this island . . ." Marquez said. She looked at J.T. He nodded, giving her his permission.

"What?" Summer asked.

"I thought maybe J.T. might have some instinct about the right place," Marquez said.

"Actually, it turned out I didn't," J.T. said, grinning crookedly.

"But . . ." Marquez took a deep breath. "Look, I don't know if this is the right time to lay this on you, Summer, but I have an idea that . . . I mean, there's all these reasons to think that . . ." She looked to J.T. again.

J.T. looked down at the ground. "Summer, I think it's possible that I am . . . your brother. I think I may be Jonathan."

Diana whistled as she poured herself a cup of coffee in a travel mug.

Her mother came into the kitchen looking early-morning grumpy. "Oh, good, you made coffee."

"Yes. I did," Diana said.

Her mother eyed her suspiciously. "You're awfully cheerful."

"Am I? Well, I'm anticipating an excellent day."

"Uh-huh. Not still angry with me?" her mother asked.

Diana smiled coolly and walked away.

"Diana, what *are* you doing?" Mallory demanded, sounding alarmed.

Diane left her behind, still yapping, and went out to her car. She drove through town and onto the highway, heading south to Key West. It really was a stunningly beautiful day, she realized. Just because almost every day was beautiful was no reason not to appreciate this one.

She pulled off the highway and into the parking lot of the state police barracks. Senator Merrick might think he owned the local police. He didn't own the *state* police.

At the front desk a sharply uniformed officer smiled at her, not quite flirting, but definitely friendly. Diana smiled back.

"What can I do for you, miss?"

"Beautiful out, isn't it?" Diana said.

"Yes, miss, it certainly is. Can I help you?"

"I'm here to report a crime," Diana said.

"Oh. What crime?"

Diana considered. "I think it's called attempted rape. Also, hitting. What's that? Like assault and battery? That, too."

The trooper's eyes grew serious. The smile was gone. "You're charging someone with attempted rape?"

"Not just someone," Diana corrected. "Ross Merrick."

"Merrick, as in—"

"Yes. *That* Merrick." Diana opened her purse and handed the trooper the videocassette. "And the really cool thing is, I have a full confession right here."

Diver sat in Summer's empty house, feeling like an intruder. It was odd how much this place seemed to belong to her now. It had been all his for a long time, till she had come.

He'd felt even stranger standing here the other day, with all three girls—Summer, Marquez, Diana. He hadn't felt right ever since. Not since he had seen *her*. She had popped up again and again in his thoughts since then, adding her own subtle influences to the troubled, uneasy feeling he now had over Summer.

He looked around. He had to admit, she'd fixed it up. There were curtains now. The smell of mildew was mostly gone. She'd put up posters and things.

He looked at the picture by her bed. He'd looked at the picture before—Summer's parents. It was an interesting picture. It showed her life when she was back in her home, what it was like there.

He hoped Summer was okay. It would be terribly sad for the people in the picture if something had happened to her. But though he had been worried all night, troubled by strange, frightening, incomprehensible dreams, he felt better now, as if somehow the light of day had chased away all fear.

The people in the picture seemed all right to him. Like Summer herself. The house in the background looked pleasant, as well. A yard. A badminton net. A barbecue grill. Grass. A nice place to play.

A place where a kid could play ball.

With a red ball.

*The first title in the fabulous
MAKING WAVES series:*

Summer and **Seth** seem made for each other –
except that **Seth** already has **Lianne.** Then
Adam falls for **Summer** too, but he's just
destroyed **Diana. Diver** needs no one. But is he
the one **Summer** needs most? Three boys, one
unforgettable holiday when . . .

Summer, can't choose

*The third title in the fabulous
MAKING WAVES series:*

At last **Diana's** tired of living with her dark secret. It's time to get even and **Diver** is the one who can help her. With **Summer** and **Seth** fast becoming an item, and **Marquez** getting back with **J.T.**, **Diana** knows it's time to take control of her life. Everything will change when . . .

Diana fights back

*If you've enjoyed MAKING WAVES,
you'll love MAKING OUT!*

MAKING OUT is a brilliant series about a bunch of teenagers who've grown up together on a tiny island. They think they know everything about one another . . . but they're only just beginning to find out the truth.

1. Zoey fools around
2. Jake finds out
3. Nina won't tell
4. Ben's in love
5. Claire gets caught
6. What Zoey saw
7. Lucas gets hurt
8. Aisha goes wild
9. Zoey plays games
10. Nina shapes up
11. Ben takes a chance
12. Claire can't lose
13. Don't tell Zoey
14. Aaron lets go